James Otis

Josiah in New York

Or, a coupon from the Fresh air fund

James Otis

Josiah in New York
Or, a coupon from the Fresh air fund

ISBN/EAN: 9783337419110

Printed in Europe, USA, Canada, Australia, Japan

Cover: Foto ©Andreas Hilbeck / pixelio.de

More available books at **www.hansebooks.com**

OR,

A COUPON FROM THE FRESH AIR FUND.

.

BY

JAMES OTIS,

AUTHOR OF "TOBY TYLER," "LITTLE JOE," "JACK THE HUNCH-
BACK," ETC.

———

BOSTON:

A. I. BRADLEY & CO.

1893.

CONTENTS.

iii

JOSIAH IN NEW YORK;

OR,

A COUPON FROM THE FRESH AIR FUND.

CHAPTER I.

THE SHINDLE FARM.

On this particular day an almanac would not have been needed to prove to the visitor at the Shindle Farm that winter was near at hand.

The wide-spreading trees leading from the road to the low-studded house, which made up in breadth what it lacked in height, had already put on their autumnal dress of crimson, gold, and brown, embroidered here and there with green left over from the last summer's wardrobe. The enormous barn was crowded to overflowing with fruits of the harvest. Mows were heaped high

5

with sweet-scented hay, and the corn-bins filled almost to bursting. The granaries seemed to groan under their heavy burdens, and the sleek cattle, noting the lack of grass in the pastures, looked into the building now and then with an air of satisfaction because of the ample supply of food housed for their especial benefit.

The broad fields, so lately beautified with waving grass, golden grain, and nodding plumes of vegetables, were waiting for the mantle of snow with which they were to be covered until spring should come again.

The yellow pumpkins, dotting the brown earth like nuggets of gold, were all that remained uncared for among the varied fruits of Farmer Shindle's industry.

The barn-yard fowls were fat, and looked so contented that it seemed certain they could have no forebodings of the Thanksgiving soon to come, while the sheep were comparing their new wool coats as if proud of the perfect-fitting garments.

In the roomy kitchen, whose well-scrubbed floor contrasted vividly with the bright brick hearth, were festoons of apples threaded on strings, like a Christmas-tree's pop-corn ornaments, and hung on convenient pegs by the thrifty housewife, who bent solicitously over the huge porcelain kettle wherein pumpkin rind was being converted into imitation citron.

Everything about the farm, animate or inanimate, appeared to be aware of winter's approach; and none so plainly gave evidence of this fact as did the heir of the Shindle estate, Master Josiah.

He was concluding his share of the harvest labors by tying together large bunches of herbs which were to be hung in the broad-beamed attic to serve, at no distant day, either as pleasing condiments for the table, or distasteful tea for Josiah when his stomach should rebel against too heavy a burden.

He well knew the uses to which these herbs would be put, and treated them correspondingly.

The sage and summer savory were fastened together with tender care, and a far-away look of happy anticipation came into his eyes as he thought of the Thanksgiving turkey; while the pennyroyal and thoroughwort were bound up roughly and tightly, as if he wished to avenge himself in advance on the disagreeable mixtures these herbs would form for his especial benefit.

This was to be the last of his duties on the farm for several days; and the most careless observer could have told, from his movements as well as the expression on his face, that some very decided change was near at hand.

Every few moments he ran to his room where a well-worn but serviceable leather valise stood half-packed with a miscellaneous assortment of wearing apparel and trinkets, and, after a hasty survey of the odd collection, returned to his work, each time consulting with his mother as to the possibility of a storm in the near future.

Three months previous Mr. Shindle had received as boarders from New York, five beneficiaries of the Fresh Air Fund in the persons of the Bartlett twins, their brother Tom, and Bob and little Jimmy Green.

These visitors, three of whom were too young to get into very much mischief, had spent a week at the farm; six whole days of pleasure unalloyed, save at certain intervals, and when they returned to their homes it was with the distinct understanding that Josiah should pay them a visit as soon after the harvesting was ended as might be convenient.

Master Shindle's parents had been parties to this agreement; and from the time he bade farewell to Bob and Tom at the railroad station, probably not a single day passed without his speaking of the promised visit.

He had never seen anything larger in the way of a town than Berry's Corner, where he lived, and which comprised not more than twenty buildings, including one store, a blacksmith's shop, and the post-office.

Josiah's anticipations were probably more keen than if no obstacles had arisen which threatened to prevent the long-promised visit.

A week previous Farmer Shindle discovered that there was a possibility of his being unable to go to the city at the time set by his son, because of business which called him in another direction; and for several days it seemed as if Josiah would be obliged to defer the journey.

The first arrangement was that his father should accompany him to New York, and come after him at the expiration of a week; for neither Mr. nor Mrs. Shindle believed their son could, with safety, travel so far alone.

As a matter of course the boy's disappointment was great; and, after several long and grave consultations, it was decided that if a letter could be received from either Master Bartlett or Master Green, announcing a willingness to meet him at the station in Jersey City, he should be allowed to go unattended.

Josiah himself carried the letter addressed to " Thomas Bartlett, Baker's Court, New York, N.Y.," to the post-office; and during the next three days the government employee at Berry's Corner had a very vivid idea of the responsibility of his position, for the Shindle heir visited the office at least twice in every twenty-four hours, intimating more than once that the important missive might have been sent in the wrong direction, or mislaid at that point.

Undoubtedly the postmaster felt relieved when it was possible for him to deliver the reply directed to Farmer Shindle in not particularly graceful penmanship; and Josiah was in a fever of excitement until he learned the contents.

Tom and Bob promised to be at the railroad station on the Jersey-City side of the river, awaiting the arrival of the train which would leave Berry's Corner at eleven o'clock Monday forenoon; and they assured the farmer and his wife, more forcibly than elegantly, that there was not the slightest danger in allowing Master Shindle to travel alone, because of the watchful care they would have over him at the terminus of the journey.

Finally the day came, as all days will, whether they be for good or evil, which had been set for Josiah's departure.

At eight o'clock in the morning he had scrubbed his freckled face twice in such a vigorous manner as threatened to rub off the skin, while his tow-colored hair was combed into a painful state of exactness.

Josiah was forced to complete the labor of caring for the herbs, which should have been performed on the Saturday previous; and after the last bunch had been carried into the attic he was at liberty once more to inspect his baggage with a view of again assuring himself that everything was in its proper place.

"The first thing I do after meeting Tom and Bob will be to sell them woodchuck skins," he said to his mother, as he came from his chamber arrayed in a new suit of clothes, and staggering under the weight of the huge valise. "Towser has bit one pretty bad, an' father says nobody will be crazy enough to buy them; but Bob told me there were lots of stores in New York where nothin' but fur was kept, an' of course they'll want woodchucks."

"Don't count too strongly on getting much money from that source, Josiah," his mother said mildly. "You have got three dollars, and that ought to be enough to spend in one week."

"So it will if I don't have to pay too big a price for the presents I want to get you and father."

"Don't bother about us, my son, but enjoy yourself, and we will be just as glad to see you empty-handed when Saturday comes, as if you brought half the things in the city. Give me your handkerchief so I can tie the money in one corner. Father's going to pay for the railroad-ticket, and you won't have any use for it until you get to New York."

Josiah had no intention of carrying his wealth in the manner proposed, for if Tom and Bob should see it in such a receptacle they would call him "green."

He had provided himself with the proper outfit at the expense of no small amount of time, and several of his most cherished treasures, by trading with one of the neighbor's boys for an old calf-skin wallet many sizes too large for himself or his money. There were two holes in it; but by the judicious use of glue and a piece of one of the woodchuck skins, he had repaired the damages until, in his eyes at least, the ancient pocket-book was as good as new.

There were many pennies in Josiah's hoard; and after these had been placed in the well-worn calf-skin, and the whole stowed snugly in the inside pocket of his coat, a stranger might have fancied he was slightly deformed; but this, according to the young traveler's ideas, was rather a pleasing addition, since, if the true nature of the protuberance was discovered, he would be looked upon as a capitalist.

For at least the tenth time Mrs. Shindle laid down rules governing his conduct during the six days he was to be absent from the farm.

" Don't run around in the grass and get your feet wet, unless you change your stockings at once ; and be sure to do exactly as Mrs. Bartlett tells you. Don't wade in the brooks; and you must not wear Tom's mother's life out bringing home all sorts of wild animals, as you do here. It is very well to have woodchucks, crows, and foxes in the country ; but in the city, where there is so much less room to move around, it will be terribly unhandy."

Josiah promised faithfully to heed these injunctions ; and after giving his boots one more coating of tallow, locking the unwieldy valise, and drawing his coat over the huge pocket-book, he was ready to start for the station.

As a matter of course, it was necessary to bid adieu to the pet calf, who was so well acquainted with the entire family that he did not hesitate about entering the house whenever the doors were left open ; and, strange as it may seem, the animal exhibited no signs of grief at his master's departure.

He butted his head against Josiah's stomach, intimating that he was ready for another pail of milk ; but the boy did not think it advisable to run the risk of soiling his clothes ; therefore, kissing the demonstrative calf directly between the eyes, he clambered into the wagon, which was drawn up in front of the kitchen door.

Then he leaned down from the lofty perch to kiss his mother, as she once more repeated the well-meant advice ; and, by an earnest application of the whip, the fat horses were started down the lane, while Towser ran on ahead, barking and wagging his short tail, ignorant of the fact that his master was about to undertake so long and seemingly dangerous a journey.

When the farm-house was shut out from view as the wagon turned into the highway, a very large and uncomfortable lump came into Josiah's throat; and, despite the past three months' anticipations, he began to feel sorry such a visit had ever been contemplated.

Of course he wanted to see New York, and meet Tom and Bob, as well as the twins and Jimmy ; but this leaving his mother was by no means pleasant, and it is probable he would have turned back then and there, if he could have done so without absolutely saying he was homesick, even before the farm was lost to view.

Every yard of distance traversed caused the lump in the traveler's throat to grow larger, and he was forced to shut his teeth tightly to prevent a veritable sob from escaping.

He realized now more fully than ever before what a good friend a fellow's mother is.

He was ashamed to let his father know the state of his feelings, and on arriving at the station remained suspiciously silent.

The tears were too near his eyelids to permit of speech without giving them an opportunity to flow, and he paid no attention to his best clothes as he took Towser in his arms and kissed him again and again.

Every thump of the dog's tail against his side seemed like a reproach because he was willing to go away even for so short a time; and when, with many a puff and hiss, the steaming engine brought the long train of cars to a standstill, the traveler could not even bid his father adieu.

" Be a good boy, Josiah ; don't get into mischief ; and I'll come for you bright and early Saturday."

Without replying, Josiah went quickly into the cars lest his tears should be seen ; and seating himself at the window he watched Towser, who ran back and forth on the platform in the greatest anxiety because his young master had disappeared from view.

This was not calculated to dispel the sorrow in the boy's heart ; and when the train moved away, Towser following to the very borders of the settlement, Josiah could control his feelings no longer.

Leaning his head on the window-frame, he gave full sway to grief ; and when the tears had ceased flowing sufficiently for him to look out once more, there was no familiar object in sight.

Berry's Corner was far away ; and as he thought of this fact there might have been another shower of tears if the newsboy had not thrown into the seat a package of candy with, perhaps, the well-meant advice : —

" Better buy that, bub! Only ten cents, an' a prize in every lot ! It'll kinder keep your mind off the calves you're leavin' behind."

This last remark may have been intended as a joke; but Josiah's heart was too sore to admit of his taking it as such, and he answered indignantly: —

" If you ever owned a calf as good as mine, you'd be sorry to leave him."

" Full-blooded Jersey, I suppose? Eighty to a hundred quarts of milk when you fill the pail with water?" the boy said with a chuckle of satisfaction, and then added impatiently, " Come, pay me for that candy! I can't stand here all day!"

Josiah was dimly conscious of the fact that he had not agreed to make the purchase; but the boy's tone was so peremptory that the huge pocket-book was drawn forth with no slight difficulty, much to the amusement of the candy vendor.

After this financial transaction was completed, and Josiah had opened the package only to find the cheapest of brass pins as a prize, the first attack of homesickness began to pass away.

He was angry because of having been cheated; and this fact, together with the panorama which could be seen from the window, so diverted his attention that, for the time being, he forgot both the calf and Towser.

CHAPTER II.

THE ARRIVAL.

A GLANCE at the plethoric pocket-book caused the boy on the train to feel a kindly interest in the traveler from Berry's Corner; and as a result of this one-sided friendship Josiah, in a comparatively short time, had two more brass pins with their accompaniment of candy, a roll of colored pictures, and three bananas.

If the distance had been longer, to this collection would have been added the news-agent's broken-bladed knife; for he had already begun to make overtures toward such a sale when the train rolled into the station, and the journey was at an end.

" Jersey City!" the conductor shouted, and the newsboy said imploringly : —

" Hold on a while. You'll have plenty of time :

the cars won't be pulled out for twenty minutes yet, and I've got a lot of things to trade."

Josiah paid no attention to the young man's request. His one desire was to meet Tom and Bob as soon as possible, and there was no question in his mind but that they were at this moment standing on the platform ready to receive him.

He fancied the general arrangement of the station would be similar to the one at Berry's Corner, and, therefore, anticipated but little trouble in finding his friends.

Staggering under the weight of the heavy valise, he hurried to the door, despite the news-agent's attempts to detain him, and, stepping down on the platform, looked about him in bewilderment.

Crowds of people hurrying to and fro as if their very lives depended upon reaching a certain point at a given time; trucks of baggage; odd, crate-like carts with tiny wheels, drawn by well-groomed horses, and the impatient panting of the engines, all served to confuse him greatly and frighten him not a little.

Had he been sufficiently friendly with the news-boy to have confided in him as to his intended course after leaving the cars, he might have been told that Tom and Bob could not get into the train-shed, but would be obliged to wait outside near the ferry-slip.

Since he was ignorant regarding the rules governing the waiting friends of passengers, he considered it necessary to remain exactly where he had alighted, arguing with himself that the boys might have been detained at home, and would soon arrive.

No one paid any attention to him.

Each person was bent on his or her business or pleasure; and the boy from the country, with his satchel beside him, stood looking first in one direction and then another for those who were to introduce him to city life.

When the passengers from the incoming train had alighted, many people came from the waiting-rooms to embark in the several cars which had been made ready for departure; and this change in the living current was to Josiah most perplexing.

He fancied he was in the station proper, and believed the new-comers had simply chanced to enter from the street in such large groups.

For a time he was interested in the bustle and confusion everywhere around him, and then came the thought that possibly his friends might be on the outside.

"I reckon that's where they're waitin'; an' I've been standin' here like a bump on a log, showin' folks jest how green I am."

Although Josiah was not ashamed of living at Berry's Corner, he hoped it might be possible to pass as a city boy, for he had a certain dread of appearing " countrified."

In order to prevent any possibility of this, he decided not to ask a single question relative to locations; but to follow in the direction taken by his fellow-passengers half an hour previous.

A sign-board bearing the name "Jersey City" attracted his attention; and he argued with himself that since this was the point where he was to meet the boys, he could not go astray by pursuing the path thus marked out.

The natural result was that he found himself in the street opposite Taylor's Hotel, almost deafened by the clatter of wheels, the cries of street ven-

dors, and bewildered by the apparently inextrica-
ble tangle of vehicles.

Tom and Bob were nowhere to be seen.

Standing with his back against an awning-post
and his valise at his feet, he spent another long,
weary time of waiting; but all in vain.

A feeling of utter desolation and homesickness
came over him, and he began to question whether
his proper course would not be to return to the
farm immediately.

A desire to be free from the bewildering bustle
prompted him to do so; but the wish to see the
big city of which he had heard so much, overbal-
anced the homesickness.

Two hours had elapsed since he alighted from
the train, and there was no longer any good reason
to believe his friends' non-appearance the result of
accidental delay.

They must either have forgotten the time set
for his arrival, or made some mistake as to the
station at which he would land.

"I ought to be big enough to find my way
around a city, even if I never was in one before,"
he said to himself. "I reckon 'most anybody can

tell me where Baker's Court is, an' I'll jest give Bob an' Tom a s'prise."

The longer he revolved the plan in his mind the more feasible did it seem; and when the hands of the neighboring clock pointed to half-past two, he started valiantly forward toward the entrance of the ferry-slip.

Greatly to his surprise the ticket-taker called sharply to him at the moment when his valise had become wedged across the narrow passage in such a manner that he was forced to come to a halt, much to the annoyance of a stout lady immediately behind him, who was urged forward by the throng in the rear.

"Two cents!" the man cried, tapping impatiently on the ledge in front of him, and the stout lady said quite sharply: —

"Why don't you have your money ready before coming inside, boy, and not delay people in this manner?"

"I didn't know I had to pay anything; father bought me a ticket from Berry's Corner to New York," and Josiah allowed his valise to drop dangerously near the stout lady's feet, as he began to explain more fully why he was impeding travel in such a manner.

"Never mind all that," she said irritably. "Pay the money, and let me get past!"

Josiah tried to obey both these commands at the same moment.

With one hand he seized the valise, while with the other he attempted to extricate the huge pocket-book from its resting place, succeeding only in causing the anger of the lady to increase.

In the meantime other persons were arriving, and, much against their will, were obliged to see the boat on which they had intended to take passage depart, while they were yet outside the gate.

The many commands for Josiah to "move on," "get out," and "don't stay there all day," so bewildered the boy that he remained silent and motionless as if unable to decide whether he should give his attention first to the valise or the pocket-book.

The ticket agent came to his relief by saying : —

"Step inside until you can find your money, and let the other passengers through."

Josiah understood this command, and obeyed

instantly, heeding not the angry glances which were bestowed upon him as the long-delayed throng succeeded in reaching the slip.

Then, working more leisurely, after considerable difficulty he succeeded in extricating his money from the depth of pocket and pocket-book, and paid the amount demanded.

This done, he marched on board the first boat which appeared ready to leave.

Again did the fates decide against Josiah's meeting his friends.

The boat on which he took passage was the one bound for Desbrosses Street, while Tom and Bob, if they had concluded to wait any longer on the chance of his coming, would be devoting their attention to the Courtland Street ferry.

Josiah had never been on a steamboat before; and he found very much to occupy his attention, not only on board, but in the scene upon the river.

The largest stream he had ever seen was the trout brook at Berry's Corner, and this broad expanse of water astonished him.

It was several moments before he could convince himself that he was not upon the Atlantic Ocean.

The many craft of every description darting here and there, filled him with wonder and amazement; and so interested was he in all around. that when the boat was made fast at the ferry slip on the New York side, he paid no attention to the fact of its being necessary to go ashore.

Standing at the after end of the steamer, he remained looking out over the river until one of the deck-hands asked : —

"Did you just come aboard, sonny?" intending, of course, to inquire if he was a passenger from that side of the river.

"Yes," Josiah replied, unconscious of the flight of time. "Say, is this the harbor or the bay?"

"It's the North River, sonny. Where are you bound for?"

"Well, you see, I jest come from Berry's Corner, an' am goin' to Baker's Court to visit Bob an' Tom."

The man was called away at this moment by the arrival of several heavy teams; and Josiah was so deeply occupied with the strange sights that the boat had started, and was nearly across once more before he became aware that there had been any stop made.

Then he asked one of the passengers standing near by, how long it would be before they arrived at New York.

"We are leaving that side now. Are you going to Jersey City?"

"Why, I've jest come from *there!*"

"Didn't get off, eh? So you are trying to cheat the ferry company out of two cents?"

"No, I ain't either. I paid the money before comin' aboard."

"Then you should have landed when the boat stopped."

"But what shall I do now? I want to go to New York."

"Stay here till the boat starts again, and then keep your wits about you, if you can, long enough to understand when she stops."

Josiah was beginning to realize he had made a mistake, and, in order to be certain of the proper direction, looked around for the station when the boat entered the slip.

As a matter of course, he failed to see any such

building, and in a troubled frame of mind remained leaning against the rail with his precious
valise between his feet until the deck-hand approached once more.

" Say, why don't you get off?" the man demanded.

" 'Cause I want to go to Baker's Court."

" Well, what's to hinder you?"

" Has the boat got there?"

" Got where?"

" Why, to Baker's Court."

" Look here, young feller, what are you givin'
me? Where is Baker's Court, anyhow?"

"It's where Tom an' Bob live in New York, of
course."

" We've just come from there. Now, when the
boat stops again take a sneak, do you hear?
Go over to the forward end where you can see
when she is in the dock, if you're so dumb you
can't tell whether she's movin' or not."

Josiah obeyed meekly, and when the steamer
entered the slip on the opposite side of the river he
took very good care to follow the passengers; but,
a short time later, deeply regretted having done
so.

The streets were thronged with vehicles to a greater extent than he had ever seen the streets at home, even when a circus was in town : and no one appeared to have a care whether he was crushed beneath the feet of the horses, or forced to remain on the sidewalk.

It was this apparent selfishness which struck the boy from the country more forcibly than anything he had experienced since his departure from home.

Even the ladies jostled him as he lingered on the crossings to ascertain whether the teams on the right or the left were the most likely to run him down; and the gentlemen had no hesitation in pushing him to this side or that, as best suited their convenience.

" Seems to me folks are in an awful hurry here. It must be there's somethin' goin' on. I've come to town to see all there is, an' reckon I'll foller the crowd for a while. There'll be plenty of time to find Baker's Court after I've had a look at the show."

Josiah followed the pedestrians with no slight difficulty, owing to the weight of his valise.

He failed to see any evidence of a " show," other than such as was obtainable from the shop windows.

Changing his valise from one hand to the other at short intervals, he continued on until it seemed as if several miles had been traversed, when he stopped in dismay.

" This won't do ! I'll get lost the first I know, an then there *will* be a muss ! I reckon I would have to spend as much as twenty-five cents if I wanted to stay all night in a hotel."

It was time he made some inquiries as to the location of Baker's Court, and he began by attempting to stop the next gentleman who passed.

" Get out of the way ! I have nothing for you."

" But I want " —

The gentleman had hurried on without waiting to hear the explanation, and Josiah eagerly turned to another.

In this second case he met with the same rebuff; and after attempting four times to make the necessary inquiries, it dawned upon him that he was mistaken for a beggar.

" The people here must be fools if they can't

answer a civil question," he said to himself. "I'm sure there ain't anybody up our way who wouldn't tell a feller where he oughter go."

" What's the matter, bub? " and a big, blue-coated policeman halted directly in front of Josiah.

" I wanter find Baker's Court, an' nobody'll tell me the way. They act as if I was beggin'."

" Baker's Court, eh? I wonder where that is? " the officer muttered half to himself.

" That's what I wonder, too. You see, Tom an' Bob 'greed to meet me at the station, but didn't come, an' I thought it wouldn't be much trouble to find their house."

" Where do you live? "

" At Berry's Corner, an' I'm here to stay a whole week. You see, the Bartlett twins, an' Tom an' Bob, an' Bob's brother Jimmy, was out to the farm this summer, an' said when they left if I'd come here they'd give me an awful good time, so "—

The policeman, instead of listening, was referring to a book which he had taken from his pocket; and, finding that no attention was paid to his story, Josiah ceased speaking.

" Baker's Court runs off West Broadway, and

that is a long distance from here. I reckon you'll have hard work to find it ; but after you've walked half an hour or so, ask some policeman, and he'll tell you."

"Half an hour or so!" Josiah repeated in dismay.

" Yes, I allow it will take that long, and if you don't stir yourself right lively you won't get there before dark."

Once more Josiah lifted the huge valise, and, following the direction pointed out by the officer, pursued his weary way with a heart quite as heavy as the burden in his hand, because of the possibility of being lost in the crowded streets, where, as he believed, so many terrible deeds of violence were perpetrated upon unsuspecting travelers.

CHAPTER III.

A FRIEND IN NEED.

"I OUGHTER gone home." Josiah said to himself as he trudged slowly along, his burden growing heavier each moment. "Now it begins to look as if I stood a good chance of being lost, and what'll become of me if I don't find Tom and Bob before dark?"

He made no attempt to answer his own question, but resolved to follow implicitly the directions given by the policeman, taking advantage of every opportunity to note the time, in order that he might not walk a single minute less than the full number set by the officer.

The half-hour came to an end, however, and the dark shadows of evening were beginning to lengthen, much to the young traveler's uneasiness, when he arrived at an open square, at one end of which could be seen a number of cabs, and on either side horse-car after horse-car until Josiah fancied all of these vehicles ever made had been brought here for inspection.

He halted.

It was easier to wait for a policeman than to search for one; and he remained at what he afterward learned was the junction of the Bowery and Chatham Square, a long while without seeing any guardians of the peace.

A short distance below his halting-place, gaudy transparencies already lighted up the dime museums, and along the edge of the sidewalk was a row of street vendors, who were crying their wares in such a variety of tones as to make a most dis-. cordant noise.

The night was fast approaching.

It was necessary Josiah should ask some one to direct him to his friend's home.

He was on the point of speaking with an Italian chestnut vendor, when a tiny girl, hardly more than ten years of age, clad in a ragged dress which had originally been brown, with the remains of a faded shawl over her shoulders, and the veriest

apology of a straw hat on her head, stepped in
front of him as she asked : —

"Don't you want to buy some matches?"

Josiah dropped his valise and looked at her in
astonishment. That a child so small should be
out on the street at such an hour, was quite as
surprising to him as that she should be insuffi-
ciently clad on a night when thick clothing seemed
an absolute necessity.

He stood gazing at her as if she was some curiosity which had escaped from the museum below,
until she repeated the question, and then he replied gravely : —

"I don't believe so; you see, I haven't learned to
smoke, an' what would I do with 'em?"

The girl continued her search for customers,
Josiah watching her intently, forgetting for the
time being his own forlorn condition as he noted
the many efforts and equally as many failures to
dispose of her wares.

Ten minutes passed, and she had not sold a single box.

Just for an instant there was a lull in the living tide, and the child had again approached

Josiah, but without paying any attention to him.

"Do you sell matches all the time?" he asked.

"That's what I have to do now. I tried to get into the newspaper business, but didn't dare to jump on an' off the cars same as the boys do, so couldn't make very much at it."

"It don't strike me you're earnin' a great sight of money at what you're doin' now. Haven't sold a thing since I've been standin' here."

"No," she said with a half-suppressed sigh, "somehow people don't seem to want to buy matches on the street. I got rid of ten cents' worth to one man, though, this afternoon.'

"How much profit was there in the trade?"

The girl looked up at Josiah inquiringly.

The boy repeated his question in another form.

"How much money did you make when you sold that lot?"

"Oh! I get a couple of boxes for one cent an' sell 'em for two, so half I take in is mine."

"Do your folks live 'round here?"

"I haven't got any. If I had I don't reckon I'd be sellin' matches."

" I s'pose you live somewhere, though ? "

" Oh, yes, old Mother Hunter lets me stay to her house for fifty cents a week."

" S'pose you don't have money enough to pay her ? "

" Then I guess she'd make me leave, same as Miss Spear did."

" Who's Miss Spear ? "

" She's the woman I went to live with when mother died, and 'twas an awful place. She used to drink terrible, an' two or three times gave me a downright good whippin' 'cause I didn't bring home as much money as she thought I oughter make."

" What right did she have to whip you? She ain't any relation, is she ? "

" Of course not; but you see I was livin' with her, an' had to pay what I promised, though when trade was good she used to want more. So I got a chance to go with Mother Hunter."

" Do you like this sort of business ? "

" Indeed I don't."

" Why not try something else ? "

" I wish I could. I thought I'd like to get a

place in a store as cash girl, but I was so small nobody wanted me, an' besides, I didn't have any
decent clothes. You see, if a girl like me gets that
kind of a job, she's got to dress up mighty fine."

"Well," Josiah said as he stepped back a few
paces and surveyed her critically, "there's one
thing certain, you ain't dressed very fine now."

"I know it," the girl said half apologetically, as
she looked down at her faded gown; "but when a
feller's got on the best she owns, what you goin'
to do 'bout it?"

Josiah was unable to answer this question. He
had never seen any one who looked so thoroughly
wretched, as far as outside appearance was concerned, not even the tramps who occasionally
stopped at the farm-house for food, and instinctively his hand went to that portion of his vest
underneath which rested the huge pocket-book.

"I haven't got much money," he said slowly, as
if weighing some important question in his mind;
"but I'll tell you what it is, little girl: I'm willin'
to give you some of it to help along, 'cause it don't
seem to me as if you was goin' to earn much of
anything to-night."

The match-girl looked at him a moment, as if determining whether he was serious in making this generous offer, and then said with what might have been a laugh : —

"If you're goin' to stay in New York very long I guess you'll need all the money you've brought, an' I must take care of myself same's I've been doin'. Say, where do you live?"

"At Berry's Corner."

"Where's that?"

"Oh, it's a good ways from here. I come in on the cars to visit Tom an' Bob. They wasn't at the station, an' I've been huntin' ever since for 'em. Looks like I was goin' to have a pretty hard job. A policeman told me to keep right on walkin' half an hour, an' then ask the way, so I reckon it wouldn't do any harm to find out if you know where Baker's Court is?"

The girl stood for an instant as if in deepest thought, and then replied slowly : —

"No, I'm sure I don't know anything about it. What street is it near?"

"The policeman said it led out of West Broadway."

"Oh, I know where that is. It may be quite a ways though, an' I wouldn't like to leave here till business was over."

" Will you go then ? "

"Of course ; there's nothin' else to do but to hang 'round Mother Hunter's, an' that ain't very pleasant."

"What's your name ? "

" Sadie Mitchell."

Just at that moment conversation was interrupted by the tide of travel, which had set in once more past that particular spot; and Sadie bent all her energies to the disposal of her wares, while Josiah looked around for a convenient place in which to remain with his satchel until the business for the day could be brought to a close.

Now that he had the promise of a guide, and one in whom he felt every confidence, he no longer had any anxiety regarding his ability to find the friends whom he proposed to visit.

Not until night had come was the girl willing to abandon her efforts toward procuring the amount of money which Mother Hunter might demand; and, despite his occupation of watching the ever chan-ging sea of faces before him, Josiah grew impatient.

"If we don't start pretty soon I'm 'fraid we won't get there before mornin'," he said, with just a shade of petulance in his tones. "Is it very much of a walk from here?"

"It might be, an' then again it mightn't. You see, I don't know how far out West Broadway it is. I'd have started sooner; but it's been dreadful hard sellin' matches to-night, an' I expect there'll be an awful row when I get home."

"When are you goin'?"

"Now; but I must stop into the house just a minute before we try to find Baker's Court."

"When will you get supper?"

"Oh I'll run across somethin' by an' by. I don't s'pose Mother Hunter's got much of anything, so it won't take me long to do my eatin'."

Josiah, who had been accustomed to having his meals regularly, was astonished at the indifference displayed by his new acquaintance regarding this matter; and as he looked at her critically while trying to learn whether she was attempting to make sport of him, the fact that he was decidedly hungry presented itself.

Owing to the excitment of the morning his breakfast had been a light one, and since then he had had nothing but candy with which to satisfy the cravings of his stomach.

What seemed like a very happy thought occurred to him.

"Is there any place 'round here where we could get somethin' to eat?" he asked abruptly.

"Of course. You can go to the Jim Fisk restaurant an' fill yourself up for fifteen cents; but that's a good deal of money to give for one supper. When trade's been good I sometimes pay a dime down to Mose Pearson's for a great big bowl of soup, an' as much bread an' butter as I want."

Josiah was silent a moment, and then said with the air of one who has fully decided an important matter: —

"Look here, Sadie, if you an' I can get a big supper for fifteen cents, we're goin' to have it, though it will make me kinder short on the presents I was thinkin' of buyin' for father an' mother; but they won't care when I tell 'em how I spent it."

The match-girl's eyes opened wide with astonishment and delight.

"Do you really mean that?" she asked, evidently

fancying he was making sport of her, and then added almost in the same breath, "I don't think you'd better do anything of the kind. It's too much to put out jest for the sake of swellin'."

"I guess I can stand it," Josiah said loftily. "I never was to the city before, an' it ain't likely's I shall get here again very soon, so we'll make the most of it while I'm on a good time. Besides, I must have somethin' to eat. an' I want you to stay with me so's to show me where Tom an' Bob live."

Sadie made no further objection, for to have spread before her a fifteen-cent meal at the Jim Fisk restaurant seemed the acme of happiness.

"What will I do with my matches?" she asked.

"You haven't got so many but I can put 'em in my pocket."

"An' I'll carry the tray in my hand. You see, if I'm goin' there with you I wouldn't like folks to think I'd been standin' out here since mornin' sellin' matches, an' was blowin' in all I'd made."

"There's no danger of that; they'll believe we just come from the country, an' have got more money than we know what to do with," Josiah said with a consequential air as he lifted the heavy valise, and stood waiting for Sadie to lead the way.

With the prospect of such a meal before her the match-girl did not delay; and as soon as Josiah signified that he was ready, she started toward Chatham Street at a pace which caused the boy, burdened as he was, no slight difficulty to equal.

Both the young people were a little timid at entering such a magnificent establishment as this restaurant appeared to be; but, aided by one of the waiters, for business was not very brisk just at this time, they were soon seated at a table which might have looked more inviting had it been less conspicuous for coffee stains on the cloth.

"What do you want?" the waiter asked, with the air of one who is not disposed to spend too much time upon his customers.

"Bring us all you've got for fifteen cents apiece," Josiah replied; and the man repeated the order in what seemed to the boy from the country like a foreign tongue.

"Ain't this just gorgeous?" Sadie whispered when they were comparatively alone. "I never was in here but twice before, an' I'd be perfectly happy if I could always eat in such a fine place."

"You ought to come out to the farm an' see how mother gets supper," Josiah said proudly. "We always have clean table-cloths, an' the dishes ain't so heavy's these; though I don't know but the more they weigh the more they cost," he added reflectively.

Then he described to her his home at Berry's Corner; told her of Towser and the pet calf, until once more the sickness for home assailed him.

The sight of the food, however, had a beneficial effect upon his mind; and in a very short time the vision of the Shindle Farm had faded away in the distance, leaving before him the pleasing knowledge that he was hungry, and had plenty with which to satisfy that desire.

To Sadie the half-hour spent in the restaurant was one of unalloyed pleasure. She thought everything around her was magnificent, and fancied that in no other place could food be prepared in such an inviting and appetizing manner.

"There!" she said as she ate the last kernel of rice which had helped to make up the pudding, and the meal was at an end, " Now I don't care what Mother Hunter says. I ain't hungry any more, an' it don't seem as if I ever will be agin. What a lucky thing for me you happened to come along, an' wanted to find your chums. I expect I'll be waitin' 'round here every night hopin' to see somebody from Berry's Corner, so's to have such an awful good time as we've had."

To Josiah the supper had not been particularly appetizing, owing to the fact that he was contrasting the food with that prepared by his mother, and the result was decidedly in favor of the meals at the Shindle Farm.

It made him very comfortable in mind that he had been able to give the little match-girl so much pleasure, however; and, after emerging from the restaurant to where the gaudy lights of the dime museum could be seen, another brilliant scheme entered his mind.

" Say, how much do they charge to go in there? " he asked.

" Ten cents."

" Then we'll go."

" That will make half a dollar you've spent since

you saw me, an' it's too much for one day," Sadie
said in a whisper, as if the enormous amount terri-
fied her.

" I don't care if it's a dollar, we're goin' into that
circus," Josiah said resolutely, as he changed his
valise from one hand to the other in order to rest
his arm, and walked rapidly toward what was announced by the posters to be the " Oriental Palace
of Wonders."

CHAPTER IV.

A SYSTEMATIC SEARCH.

JOSIAH did not regret his reckless extravagance in spending twenty cents for admission to the "circus."

Without seeing the collection of alleged wonders he never could have believed so many strange and odd things ever had an existence, and not until fully two hours had elapsed was he willing to listen to Sadie's oft-repeated assertion that it "was time to go home."

Very reluctantly he allowed himself to be led out of the building, and once on the sidewalk again found it necessary to place the valise on the curb in order that he might the better free his mind.

"Well, I declare! It beats anything I ever saw or heard tell of! Do you s'pose that fat woman could be all alive, or was she blowed up the way we do toads out our way?"

"She was a truly woman," Sadie replied. "I used to know where one of them kind of people lived, an' she was so big she couldn't hardly get into a hoss car. If you want to see a dime show that's better'n this one, you oughter go up on the Bowery. All the boys say it's just gorgeous."

"When I sell my woodchuck skins I'll go, an' you shall come along too. We'll stay all the afternoon, 'cause Bob an' Tom'll be with us, an' I reckon they'll want to see it as much as I do."

Sadie made no reply to this generous proposition, possibly because she did not believe it would ever be carried into effect; and Josiah, taking up his valise once more, followed as she led him toward Mother Hunter's.

Now that the glamour of the "circus" was partially dispelled by the more prosaic appearance of surrounding objects, the boy from Berry's Corner began to question himself as to whether he had not, as his companion suggested, spent too much money.

"I s'pose mother would think I was gettin' reckless," he said to himself, "an' I reckon it comes pretty nigh bein' true ; but p'rhaps the woodchuck skins will bring a good price, so it won't make very much difference after all. I guess I'd better sell 'em before I go to that other show."

Having thus quieted his conscience, Josiah was enabled to take more heed of his own movements, and asked his companion : —

" How far do you live from here ? "

" It's quite a walk ; but you see I want to go there before we begin to find Baker's Court, 'cause I don't know where the place is, an' it may take us a good while. Mother Hunter will be jest ravin' if I ain't back to give her some money pretty soon."

" How much have you got for her ? "

" Eight cents."

" That won't buy a great deal."

" It'll be better'n nothin', an' kinder keep her quiet. If she knows I ain't got any more she can't say very much, though she does raise awful rows when I don't bring home enough to pay for fillin' her bottle."

" What bottle ? "

"The one she drinks from, of course. She gets terrible drunk sometimes, an' lays right down on the floor."

"An' do you stay in the house then?" Josiah asked.

"Of course. Where else could I go? You see, that is my home so long as I pay what she asks, an' it's got to be there or on the street, though I did walk 'round one night when she was on a tantrum."

Josiah was shocked. He knew that at Berry's Corner on certain occasions, Daniel Downs was known to be intoxicated, and it always caused a great deal of excitement in the little settlement: but that women could so far demean themselves had never entered his mind, and more than once he decided Sadie must be mistaken.

It was destined he should have positive proof of the truth of the statement; for when they arrived at the building, and after he had followed her through an unlighted hall to as wretched a room as he had ever seen, the girl stood pointing to what at first looked like a bundle of rags on the floor.

"There she is! She must have been out beggin',
'cause I know there wasn't any money in the house
when I left."

One hasty glance at the unconscious woman was
sufficient for the boy from the country, and, turning away to avoid looking at her, he asked Sadie : —

"Now what are you goin' to do?"

"Try to find your chums, of course."

"I mean after that?"

"Why, I'm comin' back here."

"An' stay all night in the same room with her?"

"Cert; what else could I do?"

"Well, I'm sure I can't tell," Josiah replied
as he rubbed his chin reflectively ; "but it don't
seem safe."

"Why not?"

"Nobody knows what she might do to you."

"She couldn't any more'n thump me, an' I've
got used to that since I've been livin' here."

"Do you mean to say she really whips you?"

"Well, I guess you'd think so if you should see
her. She throws things, an' knocks 'round terribly
when she's gettin' over a spree ; but say, it must be
growin' late, an' if we don't hurry them fellers
won't be awake."

" I wonder what time it is ? "

" 'Bout ten o'clock."

" Ten o'clock ! " Josiah exclaimed. "Why, I never was up so late as this except once, when the sewin' circle was at our house, an' Deacon Jones an' father was talkin' so long that the deacon forgot to go home. You see, mother didn't want to send me to bed 'cause he'd think it was a hint to him. I can't go up there at this time of night."

" Then you can stay here ; there's plenty of floor," Sadie replied in a matter-of-fact tone.

" Do you lay down there when you go to bed ? "

" I can have my choice of doin' that or standin' up, so I stretch right out, an' am mighty glad of the chance most of the time."

Josiah looked around the wretched apartment, then out of the window, and back at the girl for whom he was beginning to entertain a very friendly feeling.

" I'll stay here too," he said decidedly. " I don't reckon there'll be much chance to sleep ; but that old wretch sha'n't pound you to-morrow, unless she waits till I've gone out," and Josiah laid his satchel in one corner of the room, that it might serve him as a pillow.

Sadie was perfectly willing to defer the search for Tom and Bob until morning.

This fellow from the country had treated her more kindly than the majority of her boy acquaintances; and she was well content to have him act as her guardian when the old woman, half crazed with the desire for more liquor, should begin her usual tirade.

If the worthy Mother Hunter ever owned household goods, they had all found their way to the second-hand stores or the pawnbroker's shop before this; for now one table, very shaky as to legs and with a portion of the top missing, and two dilapidated chairs, comprised the entire list of furniture.

Sadie's preparations for the night were very simple.

She curled herself in the corner opposite Josiah, pulled her hat yet farther down on her head to serve as a screen against the wind which came in through the many crevices, and said " good-night."

" Good-night," Josiah replied absently, wondering how it was that a frail girl like his new acquaintance could accustom herself to such hardships; and then, thinking more earnestly than ever before of his own rest-inviting bed with its lavender-scented sheets at home, he followed her example.

It was the first time in his life he had ever attempted to pass a night on the floor; and, despite the hardness of the boards, he slept soundly until awakened by a shrill voice raised high in threatening tones.

Springing to his feet, it was several seconds before he fully realized where he was; and then the rays of the rising sun falling directly athwart the sleeping girl, served to clear from his mind the bewilderment caused by the sudden outburst.

Mother Hunter was awake, and, if such a thing could be possible, looked even more hideous than when asleep.

She was moving excitedly about the room, calling upon Sadie in no gentle tones, and evidently searching for something which could not be found.

"Who are you?" she asked, seeing Josiah for the first time.

"I'm a feller from Berry's Corner. I met Sadie last night, an' came back here with her 'cause it was too late to find Tom an' Bob."

By this time the girl had awakened, and she said quickly : —

" It don't make any difference to you who he is. He gave me a supper, an' that's more'n I'd had if I'd come here."

" So he's got money to spend on sich as you, has he ? An' I'm starvin' to death for a drop of somethin' to warm my stomach ! " the old woman snarled.

" Well, starve then ; he won't give you anything to buy whiskey with."

" Pay what you owe me, an' that before you leave this house ! "

Sadie took the eight cents from her pocket, knowing what a refusal might cost, and gave them to the besotted wretch.

" Is that all you've got ? " the old woman cried in a rage. " Give me the whole of it, you little huzzey ! "

" That's what she made yesterday," Josiah said firmly, thinking it time he came to the rescue, " an' now she's goin' out with me."

The woman looked at him as if in surprise that he should dare speak in such a tone to her, and while she was apparently lost in amazement Josiah took advantage of the opportunity to lead Sadie from the room.

" There's no use foolin' with such a thing as that," he said, as they went through the long hall-way into the street. " The best way is to skin right out an' leave 'em alone. I reckon she'll get enough to drink with that eight cents to keep her quiet for a while, won't she? "

" It don't make any difference to me what she does, 'cause I sha'n't have to go back agin 'till night. Now we'll try to find your chums, an' then I'll go to work."

" But you haven't had breakfast yet."

" That don't make any difference; I've been without so often I've kinder got used to it."

" Well, you'll have one this mornin'; but I don't b'lieve I can afford to spend thirty cents more. S'posin' we try to find somethin' cheaper? "

" We can go 'round the corner an' get two rolls an' two sausages for five cents, if Tony has come."

" Who's Tony? "

" He's a Italian. There he is now! "

Looking in the direction indicated by Sadie,

Josiah saw a dark-skinned little man standing in front of a huge tin boiler, on the cover of which was displayed, in what was intended to be a tempting array, a collection of rolls and sausages.

In order that they might have an ample supply, the boy from the country invested ten cents, and, eating as they walked, the two turned their attention to finding Tom and Bob.

" I don't reckon they'd be at home, if they sell newspapers for a livin', 'cause it's time for the early editions already. S'pose we go down by the City Hall, an' we'll be sure to find somebody what knows 'em."

Josiah was ready to act upon any suggestion she might make, and followed her unquestioningly, after asking whether or no she was neglecting her own business by devoting so much time to him.

" Oh, no, folks don't buy matches so early in the mornin'. Plenty of time for me at ten o'clock." Sadie replied; and then, seeing a small boy on the opposite side of the street, she called loudly, " Hi ! you Sim ! Sim ! "

The boy turned in answer to her summons.

"Say, do you know the newsboys this feller's huntin' for?"

"What's their names?"

"Tom Bartlett an' Bob Green," Josiah replied.

"Know 'em? Course I do. Why, they went down town not more'n half an hour ago, an' I reckon you'll find 'em 'round the Astor House. Who is that feller, anyhow?" he added, pointing to Josiah.

"He's a boy from the country, an' is goin' to stay at Baker's Court, so we wanter find Tom an' Bob as soon as we can;" and Sadie hurried away as if time was too precious to admit of her spending many moments in conversation, while Sim muttered as he was left alone on the sidewalk:—

"Well, it kinder strikes me Sadie Mitchell's puttin' on a good many airs this mornin,' jest 'cause she's got that country Jake in tow," and the young gentleman appeared aggrieved that more information had not been given him.

"I didn't want to stop an' have a long talk," Sadie said in a low tone, when they were a short distance from Sim. "He's terrible rough. Seems as if he didn't want to do anything but jest fight.

First time he sees another feller he always puts up his 'props' as he calls it, an' I was 'fraid he might try it on you."

" I don't want to get into any row, 'cause this valise is as much as I can take care of; but I tell you what it is, these city chaps mustn't try to pick on me jest on account of my comin' from the country, for I won't stand it ; " and the young gentleman from Berry's Corner looked very fierce, as if wishing his companion to believe him a dangerous character.

Sadie was not at all alarmed by the belligerent attitude assumed by her newly-found friend, and continued on her way in search of Tom and Bob, much as though Josiah was a veritable lamb in disguise.

On the way down town the match-girl made inquiries of every acquaintance she met, regarding the whereabouts of the boys she desired to find, and received the same answer as given by Sim, except in one instance.

A young gentleman in the boot-blackening business, by the name of Jimmy Skip, informed her that he had seen the merchants in question entering a certain building devoted to offices, on Chatham Street, and stated that he had no doubt they were yet there serving their patrons.

When Sadie reached the place designated, she halted, and said to Josiah : —

" Wait here, an' I'll look for 'em. There's no need of your travelin' 'round so much while you've got that big valise."

Josiah was perfectly willing to do as she suggested, and stood leaning against the building with his burden at his feet, watching the pedestrians, an occupation of which it seemed as if he would never tire.

CHAPTER V.

A MEAN TRICK.

MASTER SHINDLE took no heed of the flight of time as he gazed around, finding something to entertain or surprise in every animate or inanimate object within his range of vision.

That which caused him the greatest astonishment, was the newsboys as they crossed the street regardless of the horses which appeared at every second on the point of trampling upon them; and when there were no longer any of these young merchants to amuse him, he turned his attention to the shop windows, where he was soon deeply interested in a collection of fire-arms.

He had long wanted to own a revolver, and it seemed to him as if now was the opportunity to purchase one, provided he received as much as he thought he had every reason to expect from the woodchuck skins; therefore it was with the air of an intended purchaser, rather than an idler, that he scanned the cards, on which was written the price affixed to each weapon.

He was still engrossed in this pleasing occupation, when Sadie's acquaintance, Sim Jones, approached, and halted suddenly on seeing him.

"There's that duffer Sadie Mitchell had in tow! I wonder what he's doin' here?" Master Jones muttered to himself, and then looked around carefully, with a view of ascertaining whether Josiah had any friends in the immediate vicinity.

There was no one near who seemed to take an interest in the country boy, and Sim concluded it was a convenient season in which to settle his debt with Sadie for not having given him more information regarding her new acquaintance.

Therefore, stepping quickly to Josiah's side, and assuming such a look as he thought would impress the stranger with an idea of his friendliness, Sim asked : —

"Say, have you found Tom Bartlett yet?"

"No; Sadie's up-stairs now lookin' for him. Some feller told her Tom an' Bob were here."

Sim gave one quick glance in at the hall, and then said hurriedly : —

" When I saw you on West Broadway I forgot to ask Sadie if you'd been over to the Mayor's office, so I hustled right 'round to find you, 'cause you see girls don't pay so much 'tention to sich things as they oughter."

" What things ? " Josiah asked in astonishment.

" What things ! " Sim repeated as if in surprise. "Do you mean to tell me you didn't know you oughter go to the Mayor's office as soon as you got inter town ? "

" Of course I didn't. What does he want with me ? "

" A mighty sight, you'll find out ! I kinder thought Sadie Mitchell wouldn't know enough to tell you, so I went 'round to the City Hall an' asked the folks if they'd seen a feller from Berry's Corner. They said ' no,' an' that the Mayor was pretty nigh wild 'cause you didn't come to him the minute you struck town."

" What does he want me for ? "

" Why 'cordin' to the law he has to give every feller from the country a dollar'n a half jest as

soon as they get here, an' if you don't skin over
there mighty quick it'll be too late."

"Tom an' Bob didn't say anything about it
when they was up to my house."

" I s'pose they thought you knowed, or else was
countin' on takin' you there as soon as you got in;
but of course it couldn't be done when they didn't
meet you.   How would it do to run over with me ?
It won't take more'n a minute, an' you'll get back
before Sadie Mitchell comes down."

Josiah hesitated an instant, and then decided
there would be no harm in accompanying this very
friendly-disposed boy, more particularly since he
seemed certain they would be back in time to meet
the match-girl, therefore he replied : —

" All right; go ahead, only we mustn't keep
Sadie waitin', 'cause it won't do for me to lose her
before I find Tom an' Bob."

" Oh, I'll look out for that part of it.   Of course
we sha'n't miss her; an' if we should. I could find
the fellers for you quicker'n she can.   It kinder
makes a boy look green to be taggin' a girl 'round
the city, an' I'm certain Tom Bartlett wouldn't
like it if he found out what you're doin'."

"It's a good deal better'n not knowin' where to go, 'cause if it hadn't been for her I'd had a pretty hard time last night, 'less I'd found Baker's Court."

While they were talking, and paying no heed to the fact that Master Jones was making sundry mysterious gestures to acquaintances whom they passed, Josiah had followed the guide from Chatham Street to Center, and not less than half a dozen disreputable looking boys were watching his every movement with the keenest anticipations of pleasure.

On arriving at what Master Shindle thought was an enormous building, because it was many sizes larger than his father's barn, Sim halted, and, pointing to the long flight of stairs leading from the street, said : —

"Go straight up there 'till you get to the top. Then open the door, an' tell the Mayor you've come for the dollar an' a half."

Josiah obeyed without hesitation, but on reaching the first landing his suspicions were aroused.

Never having visited a City Hall before, his ideas regarding one were rather vague; but he fancied the Mayor would be found in a different kind

of a place, and, despite his ignorance, the many
business signs in the hall-way soon convinced him
he was not in a municipal building.

He hesitated, turned, and was on the point of
asking for further particulars from the obliging
Sim, when he heard a roar of laughter from the
foot of the stairs.

"If the Mayor gives money to folks from the
country, I reckon Tom an' Bob would have told
me last summer," he said to himself. "That feller
is makin' a fool of me."

Then he descended to the sidewalk, and stood
looking about him in perplexity.

He had paid no particular attention to the route
taken when he left Chatham Street, and not many
seconds elapsed before the very unpleasant fact
that he was lost presented itself.

During several moments Josiah stood silent and
motionless, trying to combat the fear which came
upon him with the knowledge that he was separated
from his friends, and had no definite idea of where
they might be found.

The throng of pedestrians, each intent only on
his own business or pleasure, bewildered the boy,

and the rattle and rumble of vehicles served to increase his helplessness.

Surrounded though he was by human beings, never before had he felt so truly alone.

Involuntarily his mind went back to the time when he lost his way in the woods at Berry's Corner; but there even the birds seemed friendly, and sang and twittered about him as if to share his grief, while here no one paid the slightest attention to his sorrow, save the group of boys on the opposite side of the street, who were making merry at his expense.

Now, even more than when he caught the last glimpse of Towser's short tail at the railroad station, he wished he had never been tempted to leave the farm.

For the second time tears came very near his eyelids; but the sight of his tormentors across the street served to hold them in check, for he did not intend to allow those boys to know of the sorrow in his heart.

It was the feeling of resentment, that others should have taken advantage of his helplessness, which aided him in controlling his feelings, and he said resolutely as he walked toward Printing House Square : —

" They know I'm green as grass ; but they sha'n't see me cry."

Then turning toward the shop windows on the left in the hope of seeing one which looked familiar and thus give him some idea of his whereabouts, he pushed resolutely on until accosted by a second stranger.

" Are you the Shindle feller Tom an' Bob are lookin' for ? " the boy asked.

Josiah's short experience in the city had taught him to be suspicious, and he replied quite sharply : —

" Well, what if I am ? Are you another feller what wants to send me to the Mayor's office ? "

While speaking he glanced toward the opposite side of the street, and there saw his enemies running at full speed as if the coming of this last boy had alarmed them.

" I ain't tryin' to play any tricks," the stranger replied in a friendly tone. " Tom an' Bob are huntin' for you, an' I offered to help. Sadie Mitchell told 'em what was done last night, an' when they come out of the office they're hired to clean every mornin', you wasn't anywhere to be found. They're pretty nigh wild to know what's happened to you."

" Why didn't they meet me at the station?" Josiah asked suspiciously.

" They both went there, an' staid more'n an hour after your train got in. I happen to know, 'cause I was with 'em."

" Mighty funny," Josiah said half to himself. " I hung 'round the place two hours, an' didn't see hide nor hair of either one."

" It must be you didn't get into the right station, 'cause we watched so's you couldn't get past, no matter which door you came through."

" Why, I went right out into the street after I got tired standin' on the platform."

The stranger was silent an instant as he tried to reconcile this story with his own knowledge of the facts, and then the truth suddenly dawned upon him.

" It must have been that you didn't strike the station at all, but stood in the train-sheds till you went to Jersey City, instead of comin' 'cross the ferry."

" 'That's jest what I did."

" Then the thing is plain enough. You see, folks ain't allowed on platforms where the cars stop, an' so we had to wait near the ferry-slip. If you'd followed the other passengers it would have been all right."

" Then Tom an' Bob really was there ? "

"Of course, an' we couldn't figger out why you didn't come, 'less somethin' happened so's you had to stay at home a day longer than was 'greed on. Now, if you'll go with me, it won't take more'n half a minute to find the other fellers."

This boy spoke in a very friendly tone, and appeared to be thoroughly conversant with the matter; but at the same time it was possible he might be one of the party who had been having so much sport at the country visitor's expense.

Josiah feared the joke would be continued; but the thought came into his mind that his condition could hardly be made worse, and he replied promptly : —

"See here. I've jest come from Berry's Corner, an' never was in the city before, so don't play tricks on me 'cause I'm green."

" You needn't be afraid. I've heard what your folks did for Tom's crowd; an' if that gang over there try any funny business, I'll thump the head offer every one before night."

" I ain't sure as it's best to do that," Josiah replied hastily. " though I *should* like to get even with the feller what told me 'bout the Mayor."

" I'll give you a chance before long," the stranger said generously. " Come with me : my name's Bill Foss, an' when we've found Tom an' Bob we'll clean out that gang. They're puttin' on too many airs 'round here."

The boy turned as he spoke, and Josiah followed him, but feeling a trifle uncertain whether it would be advisable for his friends to punish the enemy very severely, because his visit was not yet ended, and he might some day find himself in a more unpleasant predicament.

"I'm a friend of Tom's," the guide said, as he slackened his pace to admit of Josiah's walking by his side. " I guess Sim Jones an' the crowd what played the trick on you know too much to fool 'round where I am."

Master Foss spoke so confidently that all Josiah's

fears fled; and when they arrived at the building where Sadie left him, he had perfect faith in Bill's integrity.

"Tom's gone over to Chatham Square lookin' for this feller, an' Bob's down to the elevated station, so you'd better stand right here till they get back," a friend of Billy's, who had been left on guard, said, as he hurried away to attend to his own business now his mission was accomplished.

In order that the time might pass pleasantly to the stranger in the city, Bill explained how he once punished a portion of that same crowd who had just played the practical joke, and while he was in the midst of the story Messrs. Bartlett and Green arrived.

Josiah had no reason to complain of the warmth of their greeting.

Each seemed to think it necessary to shake him vigorously by the hand, scrutinizing his face closely meanwhile, as if to make sure this was the same boy who had been met at Berry's Corner.

Then Josiah related his experience of the past twenty-four hours; and when he had concluded,

Tom gave an explanation similar to the one made by Bill, regarding their failure to meet him as agreed upon.

Josiah could not fail to be satisfied that his friends had kept their promise to the letter, and that it was his ignorance rather than their neglect which prevented a meeting at the proper time and the proper place.

" Where's Sadie ? " he asked, suddenly remembering that she should have been with the party.

" Up on the Bowery somewhere," Tom explained. " It's time for her to 'tend to business, an' she 'lowed she'd better leave, 'cause we wouldn't want a girl hangin' 'round."

" But we would ; " and Master Shindle spoke very decidedly. " She's been mighty good to me, an' I want to tell her I won't forget it."

" You'll have plenty of chance to do that. Just now we've got to go right up to the house an' straighten things out. When you didn't come yesterday, mother thought you wouldn't be here at all, an' we must tell her how it happened."

" Besides, you don't want to lug that valise 'round town," Bob added, " 'cause we're goin' to

put you through this city in great shape, an' can't
be bothered with a lot of baggage."

Although the boys appeared so eager to go home.
it was fully ten minutes before Josiah could answer
all the questions asked by them.

They wanted to know how the calf had thriven
since their visit to the farm, inquired particularly
concerning Towser, and were eager to learn what
would be the prospect for a good crop of turtles
next spring.

When Master Shindle had satisfied their curiosity
regarding every animal on the farm. Tom asked
with mild solicitude after Mr. and Mrs. Shindle.

The visitor was also called upon to tell how
many days he had spent weeding carrots, if the
harvest had been plentiful. and whether woodchucks allowed themselves to be killed as readily
as Josiah had intimated during the previous summer.

Then he in turn learned all that could be told
in a brief way regarding the twins and Jimmy, and
the benefit resulting from their visit to Berry's
Corner.

"It seems like as if they'd kept right on growin'

fat jest thinkin' of the farm," Tom said. "Bob
an' me promised they should go out agin before
the cold weather came, but business was dull, an'
we couldn't scrape up cash enough to pay the
fares. We're comin' next summer, though. How
many woodchucks did you kill?"

"Four; an' thousands of 'em showed up after
you fellers went away, but me an' Towser didn't
have time to get many. It was awful hard work
to tan the skins. Say, where do you s'pose I
could sell 'em? I kinder 'lowed to buy mother an'
father a present with what I got for the fur, an'
spent so much last night I don't know but it'll
take all I've got to see me through. It's dreadful
expensive goin' 'round the city, ain't it?"

"I reckon you can sell 'em at the fur stores on
Broadway," Tom replied. "The folks there buy
all kind of sich things, an' we'll see 'em to-morrow.
I s'pose you count on gettin' a pretty good price?"

"I'd be willin' to take a dollar apiece, if they
couldn't pay any more; but these are awful big
skins. It seems as if the lot oughter fetch five
dollars anyhow."

Neither of the young gentlemen from Baker's

Court was very well informed as to the value of fur; and since they had never seen a woodchuck, no idea of the market-price could be formed.

However, both were positive such pelts would sell readily, and with this assurance Josiah was content.

CHAPTER VI.

A THEATRE PARTY.

AGAIN Tom remembered that it was necessary his mother should be informed of the long-expected visitor's arrival, and he said impatiently : —

"Come on, let's go to the house now, or the folks will think you ain't comin'."

Bill Foss was obliged to attend to his regular business, and left the party as they started up town.

While the boys walked hurriedly on in the direction of Baker's Court, Josiah was suddenly reminded of a very important duty, and exclaimed as he halted in a convenient door-way : —

"Well, there ! I most forgot I had some things in this valise for you fellers !"

The curiosity of the boys was aroused, and Tom asked excitedly : —

"What did you bring? Let's look at 'em now, 'cause it'll be a good while before we get home."

Master Shindle saw no impropriety in unpacking his baggage thus publicly, and, without further urging, opened the huge valise.

"Here's what I brought you," he said, handing Tom a package wrapped in newspaper, and tied securely with several strings.

Tom unrolled the bulky parcel, removing layer after layer of paper until he brought to view a small but very lively mud turtle, which protruded its head and legs in the most engaging manner.

"Now, that's the kind of a feller what'll foller you 'round the streets," Josiah said as he held up the shell that his companions might observe more closely the reptile's beautiful proportions. "Tame him right. an' I guess he'll be most as good as a dog, though he can't go very fast."

As Tom took the pet. Josiah again plunged his hand into the valise. this time bringing forth a small wooden box, which he gave to Bob as he said : —

"I was goin' to fetch two ; but didn't dare to

put em together, an' there wasn't room enough
in the valise for another box."

Opening the lid Bob saw a small green snake,
which lifted its head and gazed around inquiringly,
as if asking why it had been thus suddenly transported from its home to a place where there was
no opportunity of hiding.

Bob thanked his friend for the gift, but looked
so longingly toward the turtle that Master Shindle
hastened to say : —

"If you'd rather have one of them I can catch
more'n a thousand when I get home agin ; but
seein's how they're apt to bite babies, an' you've
got the twins an' Jimmy 'round, I didn't know as
it would do to fetch two."

"If you'll send 'em down, I'll pay the freight,"
Bob replied ; and Josiah promised that on the day
following his return home he would capture as
many turtles as his friends might desire.

Then he displayed the gifts intended for the
twins and Jimmy, — two last-year's bird's nests, a
large supply of horse-hair as materials for rings
and chains, and a collection of hedge-hog quills
which his mother had dyed in various colors.

After these had been inspected and duly admired, the boys continued on their way to the court, walking very slowly because of Josiah's desire to stop and look at everything around him.

More than once his exclamations of surprise attracted a crowd of newsboys and boot-blacks; but Tom and Bob were careful to prevent him from being annoyed by these young gentlemen, who considered a stranger from the country a fair target for their supposed wit. and Josiah continued slowly on, ignorant of the fact that he was affording others quite as much amusement as he received from the novel scenes.

Under ordinary circumstances, Tom and Bob could have walked from Chatham Square to their home in ten minutes; but on this day it was fully an hour before they arrived at the court, although both hurried Josiah as much as possible by promising to show him all these things and many more, later in the day.

On entering the court Master Shindle looked about him in dismay; and Bob, quick to note the change in the expression of his friend's face, said with a laugh : —

"Doesn't seem much like the farm, eh? I told you one week in a place like this would be enough. If you had always lived here, it wouldn't look so dirty; but you'd be as wild as we were to see the country."

"Oh, this is nice," Josiah said quickly, fearing lest his friends might think he was making invidious comparisons; and just then the twins and Jimmy came running up to greet their host of the previous summer, thus bringing to a speedy conclusion what might have been a very awkward conversation.

The dilapidated houses, and the clothes hanging on lines from one side of the court to the other, as if to shut out the light of the sun, gave to Josiah a feeling of homesickness similar to that which he had felt when catching a last glimpse of Towser.

To remain on the principal streets where he could look in the shop windows, or on the water-front and gaze at the vessels, would have been pleasant; but there was such a wide difference between the buildings of Baker's Court and the Shindle farm-house, that he would have been quite contented had he known his father was coming after him that same day.

Mrs. Bartlett and Mrs. Green received him cordially, and yet he was far from being comfortable in mind.

The small, stuffy kitchen was not like his mother's, and he could hardly believe food coming from it would taste as sweet.

The room which he was to share with Bob and Tom was far from being as inviting as his own; and the air, although it was late in the season, seemed oppressively warm.

Very likely Tom and Bob would have made almost the same comparisons in favor of the farm; but Josiah tried earnestly to prevent any show of discontent, and, after doing full justice to the lunch hastily prepared by Mrs. Bartlett, the boys went into the street once more, leaving behind the twins and Jimmy to play with the hedgehog quills at imminent risk of injuring their eyes, or making painful punctures in their skin.

Once in the business portion of the city again, there was so much to attract Josiah's attention that he entirely forgot the disagreeable impressions of the court; and the three flitted about from window to window to the delight of Master Shindle and the perplexity of his hosts, who found it extremely difficult to keep at a respectful distance the numerous acquaintances who followed in the hope of having some sport at the expense of the boy from the country.

"That is great!" he said when Tom and Bob gave in detail the programme they had arranged for his entertainment.

The party was to visit Coney Island, the park, and, as a rare treat, it had been decided to spend that very evening at the theatre, to which end three gallery tickets had already been purchased.

This last announcement excited Josiah for the moment so that he lost all interest in the novel sights around him.

He had heard of the theatre; for Sam Perry knew a boy living about seven miles from Berry's Corner who had really been inside such a place, and Josiah was willing to confess that no other form of entertainment could afford him so many pleasurable anticipations.

The sight-seeing, and the promise of the delightful excitement which was yet to come, did not prevent Josiah from remembering the first friend he had made in the city, and he asked anxiously : —

"Is Sadie goin' with us?"

"Of course not. We don't want a girl taggin' 'round, an' I reckon she wouldn't care to go very much."

"Oh, yes she would, 'cause she thought it was awful nice at the circus."

"Circus!" Bob repeated in surprise. "Where have you seen one?"

"She an' I went the evenin' I was tryin' to find you. It's down a little ways from where she sells matches."

"Oh, that's the dime museum, an' don't 'mount to much longside of one up on the Bowery. We can go to them kind of places any day;" and Master Green spoke as if half the marvels of the earth were gathered at this particular place, but yet were hardly worth the attention of himself and his friends.

"But I'd like to see her again. She was mighty good to me."

"There'll be plenty of chances for that when we have nothin' else to do. We'll skin up 'round Broadway, an' then go home, for it'll be pretty near supper time when we get there."

" Well, I don't want to make any mistake about seein' her agin, 'cause I ain't really squared up for the way she treated me ; an', besides, I'd like to be certain she's havin' as good a time as I am, for, 'cordin' to the looks of things, she gets it pretty tough."

" That's a fact," Bob replied. " It must come kinder hard on anybody what has to live with Mother Hunter: but I reckon she's got used to it. Anyhow, you shall see her to-morrow if that'll do any good."

" An' will you take her with us to some of the places if I pay the bills?"

" Yes," Bob replied slowly, but in a tone of indecision, " I s'pose we can fix it somehow:" and with this rather unwilling promise the subject was dropped for the time being.

It was so difficult to tear Master Shindle away from the shop windows that the evening meal had been ready nearly an hour when they finally arrived at Baker's Court.

In the stuffy little kitchen, which also served as a dining-room, Josiah had once more an opportunity of comparing his home with this, and for at least the tenth time decided that life in the city was entirely different from what it had been pictured by some of his acquaintances at Berry's Corner.

Instead of an accompaniment to the meal by a bird orchestra, they had the rumble and clatter of carts in the street; in lieu of the perfume of flowers which swept through his mother's quaint kitchen, was an unpleasant odor from the court, and he ceased to wonder that the beneficiaries of the Fresh Air Fund found the farm such a pleasant abiding place.

There was but little opportunity for reflection on this subject, however. The meal was eaten hurriedly that they might arrive at the place of entertainment before the doors were opened, in order to make certain of obtaining front seats, therefore not a moment was wasted.

Josiah's remembrance of this visit is not altogether pleasant.

During fully three-quarters of an hour he stood with a large number of boys in the narrow hall-way, pushed here and there until it seemed as if he must be literally flattened like a wafer.

When the doors were finally opened he was borne by very press of numbers up three flights of dimly-lighted stairs into a not over-cleanly place, which was considerably warmer than the carrot patch in July; then down a steep incline until it seemed as if he would surely be pitched from the railing to the vast pit, the bottom of which appeared to be paved with human heads.

The theatre party from Baker's Court was in the front row, with nothing to obstruct the view of a gaudily-painted piece of canvas, which covered — Josiah knew not what.

He did not speculate as to the possible wonders which might be behind it; for the noisy throng, the heated air, the odor of gas, and the loud buzz of conversation bewildered him to such an extent that he began to fear he should not be able to get away alive.

On one side Tom was telling of the wonderful things which would be revealed when the curtain was raised; and on the other Bob praised the scenery, or the daring of the hero whose brave deeds were to be portrayed, while Josiah listened without understanding a single word.

Then, after much stamping of feet, whistling and cat-calls, came a burst of music, and the visitor from the country began to feel more at his ease.

With elbows resting on the wooden railing, and both hands held behind his ears that not a single note from the noisy orchestra should escape, he gave himself up wholly to what he supposed was the performance, wondering not a little why Tom and Bob had said so much about hair-breadth escapes, when he could see nothing more dangerous than the brass instrument which a musician lengthened and shortened until there seemed every fear he would decapitate his neighbor.

" Is he goin' to kill the man next to him with that brass thing ? " Josiah asked in a hoarse whisper.

" Of course not," Bob replied scornfully ; " that is only one of the orchestry, an' don't 'mount to anything. Wait 'till the curtain goes up, an' then your eyes'll stick out ! "

Josiah waited simply because he was forced to do so ; and when the performance began, exclamations of surprise and astonishment burst from his lips, as what appeared to be a veritable forest was suddenly unfolded to view.

During the three hours which followed he remained in a daze of wonder, fear, and bewilderment.

He could not understand why at one time there was a forest behind the curtain, and at another the interior of a house, therefore this sudden change confused him.

It was impossible to hear every word spoken on the stage, and, consequently, he failed to comprehend why people ran around discharging fire-arms so frequently.

Owing to these drawbacks the performance was not as pleasing as it might have been, while the heat, lack of ventilation, and the general excitement, gave him a most severe headache.

Therefore, instead of regretting that the evening's entertainment had come to an end, as did Tom and Bob, he was only too well satisfied to be in the comparatively fresh air once more.

"To-morrow mornin' we'll go up to the park," Tom said as they walked rapidly toward Baker's Court; for he fancied, because of his friend's silence, that the boy from the country was having another attack of homesickness.

This supposition was correct; and when Josiah was in the tiny chamber he would have been perfectly willing to bring his visit to an immediate close, if by such a means he could be transported instantly to his own room, where his mother would be within call.

CHAPTER VII.

A MIDNIGHT ALARM.

THE labor of sight-seeing had so wearied Josiah that his eyes closed very quickly after getting into bed, despite the unpleasantness of his surroundings; and he did not return from dreamland until at an early hour next morning, when the sudden clash of heavy wheels, the clang of gongs, and the hoarse rush of escaping steam, brought him from the bed to his feet trembling with undefined fear.

"Hurry up and get into your clothes!" Tom cried. "There's a fire, an' it sounds as if it was right here in the court."

Josiah's only experience in such matters had been when Deacon Fuller's barn burned, and he and his father watched it, unable to do anything toward fighting the flames because of lack of water.

Therefore he was thoroughly alarmed, believing

Tom's home would be destroyed, and these fears caused him to be awkward in making his toilet.

At first he could not find his clothes; and when this had been finally accomplished, it seemed impossible to get them on. After what appeared to be a very long while he succeeded in dressing himself, and, seizing the heavy valise, followed Bob and Tom, who had already begun to descend the stairs.

The heavy panting of the engines, the firemen's hoarse commands, and the running to and fro of people who were pouring from the tenements of the court, made a most terrific din.

Here and there great fiery eyes stared out of the darkness, causing those who passed in front of them to look like shadowy giants, while the network of hose extending in every direction, and from which tiny streams of water were spurting, formed for the country boy a picture which was not less alarming than bewildering.

" The fire's on the other side of the street," Tom said a moment later, " an' I guess there ain't any chance the court will be burned, but it makes a good show if you never saw such a thing in the city before."

Josiah looked in vain for the flames.

The glowing furnaces of the engines seemed to him more dangerous than any hidden conflagration could possibly be; and in fear and trembling he stood behind his companions, pressing close against the wall of a building, until Tom chanced to see the heavy burden he was carrying.

" What did you bring that valise for ? " he asked, laughing heartily.

" I'd rather have it in my hands if the house is goin' to be burned," Josiah replied timidly ; and then, after no little urging, Tom succeeded in inducing him to give up the valuable baggage that he might carry it back, while Bob, with a bravery which the boy from the country thought foolhardiness, made his way among the panting engines in order to show his guest the method of fighting fire in the city.

It was not such an investigation as pleased Josiah, this going to and fro among the monsters which swayed back and forth under the pressure of steam as if about to explode, and being treated to frequent shower-baths from the leaking hose, or almost overturned as the busy firemen rushed past.

Even before Tom returned he persuaded Bob to go back to the court where they might at least be in a place of comparative safety.

During half an hour he remained gazing at the building which was supposed to be food for the flames, and then the din lessened.

One by one the heavy, noisy machines were drawn away, the serpent-like lengths of hose were rolled on the carriages, and when Tom announced that the fire was extinguished, Josiah was even more mystified than before.

"That's the funniest kind of a fire I ever saw," he said as they returned to their room, debating whether it would be best to retire once more, or dress themselves for the day's pleasuring, for the shadows of night had already given way before the coming dawn. "At Berry's Corner people have to carry water in buckets."

"It ain't very often you have a chance to see a fire in the city, 'cause the engines get to work so quick," Bob explained; and then he told of a conflagration near the docks which he and Bob had seen, until by the time the story was finished Mrs. Bartlett called them to breakfast.

After the meal was brought to a close, Josiah wished to visit Chatham Square in the hope of seeing Sadie; but Tom and Bob decided against anything of the kind.

They had planned to spend this day in Central Park; and, despite Josiah's desire to meet the girl who had been so kind to him, he was obliged to accompany his friends, or be guilty of rudeness by questioning their judgment in preparing a programme which was intended for his especial benefit.

"You see, it don't look very nice to be runnin' 'round with a girl, an' the fellers will make all kind of fun of you," Bob said in a fatherly tone. "Of course, if we're anywhere near Chatham Square it's no harm to go an' talk with her; but this pullin' Sadie along with us everywhere ain't the right way at all. Things are different in the city, you know, from what they are in the country."

"Yes, I know," Josiah replied mildly; "but you see she was so awful good to me when I lost my way an' was feelin' bad, that it don't seem as if I could do too much to square things up with her.

It ain't likely she gets a chance to go off on such times very often."

"I don't reckon she does," Tom replied; "but she can't count on stayin' with us, 'cause it would spoil all the fun to begin with, an' then agin, no feller could help laughin' if he saw her with us. We wanter go by ourselves, an' do the thing up in style, that's what we're after."

"I won't talk any more about it now," Josiah said; "but I've got to see her again before I go home."

"There'll be plenty of chance for that. She's allers up there sellin' matches. When we haven't got anything better to do, Bob an' I'll go with you. Now come on, 'cause we wanter scoop in all we can."

Josiah followed his friends out of the dirty court into the noisy street, and down to the Sixth Avenue elevated railway station, where he clambered up the stairs with no slight degree of trepidation, for this "goin' on the roof to find a train of cars" was something so novel in his experience as to be almost alarming.

First he feared the stair-way was not sufficiently

strong to bear in safety all the people crowded upon it, and then he began to feel quite positive the small pillars which upheld the tracks would be crushed beneath the weight of the train.

Tom and Bob enjoyed his nervousness.

Previous to this time they had failed to show their guest anything which impressed him quite as much as they desired : but now their efforts were crowned with success, and it was in the highest degree satisfactory to them.

"I would have been willin' to pay ten cents rather than not seen him fidget 'round as he's doin' now," Tom whispered to Bob as Josiah, standing near the news-counter, shrank back from the edge of the platform lest he should be thrown into the street by the throng of passengers around him.

Josiah managed to hide his fears after a few moments, greatly to the disappointment of his friends ; and when he entered the cars there was no thought of the match-girl, for this being able to look in at the second or third story windows of the buildings which they passed was something so strange that there was no room in his mind for anything else.

"I'll bet Tim Berry's eyes will stick out when I tell him of this ride," he said in a confidential whisper to his friends. "He never saw anything like steam-cars runnin' in the air, an' jest as likely as not won't be willin' to believe what I tell him."

"This ain't nothin' at all to what you'd see if you went up Harlem way," Bob replied. "Why, there the tracks are higher from the ground than the top of that steeple, an' it looks like as if the cars would tumble right off when she swings 'round a curve."

"Ain't we goin' there?" Josiah asked.

"I don't reckon it would pay. You know we wanter put in all the time we can in the park; but we'll see how things turn out after we're ready to go home."

Josiah was really sorry when Tom whispered that they were to leave the cars at the next station; for it seemed to him that he would be satisfied to do nothing else all day but "ride in the air," as it appeared they were now doing.

On descending to the street once more, Bob began the pleasuring by purchasing a pint of peanuts;

and, contentedly munching them, the three entered the park.

Here, to the disappointment of his hosts, Master Shindle evinced neither surprise nor delight at what he saw.

" Don't you think it's great, up here? " Bob asked, after they had walked a long distance in almost perfect silence, save for the crunching of nut-shells as they extracted the meat.

" Yes, oh yes," Josiah replied. " It's good enough for a field, I s'pose ; but it seems to me they'd make more money to put it in crops, than lay all this land down to grass, an' I notice they don't pick the rocks out. Now, if there was as big a ledge in our mowin' field as that, father'd have had it blasted in less'n no time."

" But they don't run a farm here, you know. This is only for the folks to look at," Bob explained.

" And do people travel out here jest to see a mowin' field? "

" Yes, with all the other things."

" Well, they oughter go to Berry's Corner, an' see Deacon Jones' meadow; a hundred acres, an' not a rock on it; jest as smooth as a floor. He wouldn't have these bushes on his place no more'n he'd fly."

It was not until they had arrived at the lake, and he saw the marble bridge and the playgrounds, that Josiah condescended to be more than mildly interested in the surroundings.

Then he was willing to admit that this might be more beautiful than " Deacon Jones' meadow," and Bob began to have great hopes of surprising him before the visit had come to an end.

" Jest wait till we get down where the animals are! That's what'll knock your eye out!"

As a matter of course the party indulged in a boat-ride, and after making a complete circuit of the lake three times, were ready to " take in " the zoölogical collection.

Josiah was not willing to move quite as rapidly as his friends desired.

He was deeply interested in the throngs of people around him in holiday attire, and found quite as much to amuse in the ever-changing scene near the boat-landing as he had in front of the shop windows, while Bob and Tom thought only of reaching the monkey-house that they might enjoy the antics of those animals.

"Come on! It's foolish wastin' so much time here when there's lots more to be seen," Bob said impatiently. "I thought we'd better strike this place first, an' then we could stay as long as we wanted with the animals."

"I'm comin'," Josiah replied, and during two or three moments he remained close behind his friends; but then, as the oddest kind of a vehicle, which he fancied was a stage-coach, drove past with four horses, a remarkably well-dressed driver, and a man on top who played on a long horn, he forgot the necessity of keeping very near his guides.

Now, while neither Bob nor Tom had seen so many tally-ho coaches as to treat them with indifference, this one was not so very remarkable as to cause any surprise or comment on their part; and they continued on rapidly, heeding not the fact that Josiah was still standing in open-mouthed astonishment, gazing after the swell equipage.

It was quite as easy for him to lose his guides in the park as on the city streets; and Josiah was very soon made aware of this, for when the coach was lost to view in the distance he started on in the direction he believed had been taken by his companions, but it was not possible to see them even after five minutes of rapid traveling.

"Well, I'm lost again," the boy from Berry's Corner exclaimed, as he came to a full halt. "It seems to me that's about all I'm doin' in this town; but I won't make a chump of myself by walkin' alone. I'll wait right here till they come," and he seated himself on a convenient bench, resolving to remain there as long as might be necessary.

Time did not hang heavily on his hands, owing to the vehicles which were constantly passing, thus affording him ample amusement; and it would have been impossible for him to say whether one minute or twenty had elapsed since he lost sight of his friends, when a boy, apparently several years older than himself, came toward him in an officious manner, rattling half a dozen pennies in his hands as he said sharply: —

"Well, come down with the stuff. I can't wait 'round here all day, 'cause there are too many other fellers to watch for."

"You needn't stay a single minute on my account," Josiah replied, determined not to allow himself to be deceived again, as in the case of the supposedly necessary visit to the mayor.

"Oh, don't be funny! Come down with the stuff!"

"Look here, what's the matter with you?" Josiah asked impatiently. "What do you want, anyway?"

"You don't b'long in this city, do you?" the boy asked sharply.

"Of course I don't."

"Well, then, what are you doin' up here?"

"Jest come to look 'round with Tom an' Bob."

"Do they live in town?"

"Of course. Down in Baker's Court."

"Have you got your ticket?"

"What ticket?"

"To see the park, of course. Did you pay anything when you came in here?"

"Bob paid for the peanuts, an' I whacked up for the boat-rides."

"There, now you're gettin' funny agin! You know what I want! Come, down with it; ten cents, an' do it quick too!"

"Ten cents for what?" and now Josiah began

to think this boy really had some right to address
him in such a tone.

" For lookin' at the Park."

"But Tom an' Bob invited me up here with
them."

"I can't help that. It costs ten cents to come
in, an' that's all there is to it. You wanter pay
quick, or you'll get inter trouble."

" But they didn't tell me anything 'bout it."

"They live in town. It don't cost them anything; but all fellers from the country have to pay."

Josiah looked around eagerly in the hope that
his friends might be in the immediate vicinity;
but in this he was disappointed.

He could see no one whom he thought he might
venture to ask for information, and the boy who
claimed the right to collect money for sight-seeing
was growing more and more impatient each instant.

" I'd rather wait till they come back."

" Well, you can't. I've got to go all the way
'round the lake in an hour, an' if I have such
trouble with every feller as I do with you, it'll
take me a week to fix things."

The boy was standing directly in front of Josiah

by this time, and looked so threatening that the visitor from Berry's Corner did not dare to prolong the interview.

It was with the greatest reluctance that he drew from his small hoard a dime, and, holding it between his thumb and finger as if unwilling to part with it, asked : —

" What do I get when I give you this? "

"Get? Why you have the chance of seein' all there is here. What more do you want? " and without further ceremony the alleged collector took the money from Josiah's fingers, walking rapidly away.

" Look here ! " the latter shouted. " S'pose'n somebody else comes 'round collectin' ten-cent pieces, how'll they know I've paid? "

" That'll be all right. I'm the only one at this end of the park," and the boy hurried away as if fearing some of the pedestrians might inquire the meaning of this rather odd question.

" Well, it strikes me I'm goin' it pretty stiff. It cost me fifteen cents in them boats, an' now ten more's twenty-five. If we're goin' to stay all day I sha'n't' have any money left when I get home,"

Josiah said ruefully, and just at that instant a cry from the opposite side of the driveway caused him to spring to his feet.

"Why didn't you keep close to us?" Bob asked with just a shade of petulance in his tones. "If you go to gettin' lost this way we sha'n't have any kind of a time, 'cause the whole day'll be spent huntin' for you."

"I didn't mean to," Josiah replied penitently; "but while I was lookin' at the stage you fellers got away. Say, why didn't you tell me it cost ten cents to see this park?"

"Ten cents to see this park?" Bob repeated in bewilderment.

"Yes; that's what I jest had to pay."

"Who asked you for it?" and now both the young gentlemen from Baker's Court ran quickly to the side of their friend.

Josiah related the interview which he had had with the alleged collector, and when he concluded Bob and Tom burst into a fit of laughter.

"Well, you are too green to live," Bob said as soon as it was possible for him to speak. "The idea of givin' up good money to any feller what comes along askin' for it!"

"But I had to. He was goin' to make me."

"Make nothin'! He'd been mighty careful to get away if you'd raised a row. But say, it won't do for him to go off with that ten cents. Let's hunt after him!"

Tom was quite as anxious to search for the boy who had robbed their friend; and, under the guidance of Josiah, the three started.

"Are you sure you'll know him?" Bob asked.

"Indeed I will; but say, fellers. I don't want to get into any row here jest 'cause of that money. I'd rather give twice as much than have a fuss."

"There won't be any trouble. He'll come down with the stuff as soon as we get hold of him." Tom replied confidently; and an instant later Josiah cried, as he pointed toward a group of boys standing near a statue: —

"There he is! That feller with the stick in his hand! He's the one!"

It hardly seemed advisable for the three to attempt any reprisals just at this instant.

The alleged collector had with him six other boys, who were evidently friends. and there was little question but that the effort to force him to give up his ill-gotten gains would end disastrously for the smaller party.

"It won't do to tackle him yet a while." Bob said, after mentally taking the measurements of the boy and his friends. "We'll have to wait a spell, 'cause there's too many of 'em."

"By holdin' back we may never get a chance. Jest as likely's not they'll stick together till they go home," Tom replied.

"But you'd be makin' fools of yourselves to start in now," Josiah suggested. "Wait till one of them men in the soldier clothes comes along. Then go right up an' ask for the dime. He won't dare to keep it."

This seemed to be a very good idea; and Bob was willing to act upon it provided it would not be necessary to wait too many moments, for time was of more value just then, in his opinion, than the money which had been extorted from Josiah.

Fortunately they were not delayed a great while, for Bob had hardly hidden himself behind a clump of shrubbery, before two of the park guards were seen approaching from either end of the street; and he called Tom's attention to the fact by saying : —

"Come on! Now's our time, an' we don't want the policemen to hear if we can help it, 'cause they'll make us stay as witnesses."

"Go ahead, an' I'll stand right at your back. Give it to him good and strong."

This advice was not necessary, for Bob was so thoroughly in earnest that he had no idea of "giving it" to him in any other way than "strong."

The boy who had wrongfully collected Josiah's dime saw the three as they crossed the street toward him, and, as a matter of course, recognized his victim. He turned as if to beat a hasty retreat, but, seeing the officer, wheeled once more, only to face a second guard, and then stood at bay.

"Look here, young feller, you pulled ten cents outer my friend, an' I want you to give it back to him mighty quick," Bob said sternly.

"Oh, you do, eh? S'pose you try to make me."

"I 'low it wouldn't be sich a terrible big job, anyhow; but I've got other business on hand jest now, an' I'm reckonin' you'll give it up rather'n have me tell a policeman."

For an instant it seemed as if the boy meditated resistance; and then he must have realized how useless such a course would be. for he delivered the money to Bob. as he started at full speed across the lawn. regardless of the warning signs to " keep off the grass," striking Josiah a heavy blow on the side of the head as he departed.

" Here. take your dime ! I'll thump the nose offer that feller! " Bob cried angrily. as he handed the money to Josiah. and was on the point of pursuing the enemy, when Tom caught him by the arm.

" Now. don't go to makin' a fool of yourself, 'cause they'll have you in the station-house quicker'n lightnin' if you try anything like that! Better let him go, an' say no more 'bout it."

" But what did he hit Josiah for? I ain't goin' to stand still an' let him thump my visitors."

" You can't help yourself, now it's done. It's only a case of gettin' inter trouble if you keep on this way," Tom said sharply. and Josiah added : —

" Don't pay any attention to him. Bob. It didn't hurt me so very much. an' I oughter got it worse'n that for bein' so mighty green."

It was with difficulty that Master Green restrained his anger, and perhaps he might not have

been able to do so but for the fact that Tom
reminded him they were wasting time which should
be spent viewing the animals; therefore he contented himself by saying threateningly : —

"I'll lay for that feller. Jest as likely's not
we'll catch him down town sometime, an' then
he'll find out whether he can come 'round stealin'
money, an' knocking the heads offer fellers without
gettin' as good as he sends, or not."

"That's the style! Wait till we get him on our
own ground, an' then pay him up. Now come on :
we've fooled more'n an hour away, an' before you
know what's what it'll be time to go home."

Then, without waiting to parley further, Tom
started off in the direction of the zoölogical collection, and his companions could do no less than
follow.

CHAPTER VIII.

THE ZOÖLOGICAL COLLECTION.

EVEN if the bogus collector of admissions to Central Park had dealt him a much heavier blow than really was the case. Josiah would have forgotten about the injury entirely, in the amazement and delight with which he viewed the inmates of the monkey-cage.

Never but once before had he seen any of these long-tailed animals; and that single occasion was when an organ-grinder, with such a companion, visited Berry's Corner, to the intense delight of the younger portion of the population, and the annoyance of their elders.

But that monkey, held by a chain, and buckled into a coat so small that he could hardly breathe, was an entirely different sort of an animal from those who were revelling in the semi-freedom of the cage; and it seemed to Josiah as if he would never weary of looking at them.

With a reckless disregard of the amount of money on hand, and an utter forgetfulness of the presents which he wished to carry home to his parents, Josiah purchased peanuts and cookies for the purpose of feeding the occupants of the monkey-house, until there was every danger his supply of ready cash would be entirely exhausted.

What seemed to him quite remarkable was the fact that so many of the animals resembled certain inhabitants of Berry's Corner.

More than once he called the attention of his friends to a striking likeness between these creatures and some of his acquaintances, and repeated over and over again that he would be willing to cut his visit very much shorter than had originally been intended, if by so doing his father and mother could see the wonderful antics of the agile animals.

Bob and Tom were forced to literally drag him away from the entrancing scene, in order to prevent complete bankruptcy: and even though not less than two hours had been spent in this particular building, it seemed to him as if he had hardly entered before he was outside once more.

His friends had led him in turn to where the elephants, buffaloes, and bears could be seen, and at each enclosure he made the same remark : —

"I'd rather stay in the monkey-house, than go all over this park a dozen times:" and since their sole purpose was to afford him amusement, it became necessary to allow him to return to the spot where, in his mind, was centred the chief attraction of Central Park.

Not until nearly night-fall was he willing to drag himself away from this delightful occupation : and even then it is barely possible he might have made some protest against departure, but for the fact that the buildings were being closed for the evening.

With a long-drawn sigh he walked slowly on with his companions, and as the distance between himself and the prototypes of Berry's Corner's most distinguished citizens was increased, he began to think of his rapidly decreasing capital.

"I tell you it costs somethin' to live in the city," he said, instinctively placing his hand over the shrunken pocket-book. "Why, at home I can't get a chance to spend a dollar in a month : but here

it seems as if it was pourin' out all the time.
I don't know what'll become of me if I stay a great
while."

"When a feller's on a spree money goes pretty
fast." Master Bartlett replied philosophically.
"But you've still got the woodchuck skins to sell,
an' they oughter bring a good price. We'll tend
to 'em in the mornin'."

"It'll come kinder hard on me if I don't get
somewhere near what I've been figgerin' on,"
Josiah said thoughtfully. "'cause I've been goin'
it mighty strong since I struck this town."

"You mustn't bother your head 'bout that. You
don't come down here so very often, an' can 'ford
to blow yourself pretty well when you do strike
the city. A hundred years from now it won't
make any difference."

"I ain't lookin' ahead so far as that," Josiah
replied grimly. "The hundred-year part of it'll
be all right; but I'm thinkin' 'bout the balance of
this week."

"We'll see you through;" and then Tom dis-
missed the matter, as if advancing his friend several
dollars would be nothing more than an ordinary

business transaction to which he was thoroughly well accustomed.

The ride down town in the elevated cars was not as pleasant as the one in the morning had been, owing to the fact that it was now dark, and there was less to be seen, while the visitor was decidedly tired.

The walk from the station to Baker's Court seemed unusually long, and the supper, even though it was served in the stuffy kitchen, was appreciated to its fullest extent.

Had Josiah consulted his own inclination, he would have retired immediately after the evening meal was brought to a close; but Bob and Tom were eager their friend should view Brooklyn Bridge in the night, when the lights of the city formed a brilliant background, and almost reluctantly Josiah allowed himself to be conducted from the court once more.

" By gracious! If I get used up walkin' 'round havin' a good time, what must it be for that little match-girl, who's on her feet all day, an' with not half enough to eat?"

" Well, it's tough, of course," Tom said thoughtfully ; " but there's a good many of us got the same kind of a snap, an' I don't reckon she's any worse off than lots I could pick up."

" S'pose she's had any supper to-night ? "

" Now see here, Josiah," and Tom spoke very decidedly. " It's no kind of use for you to spoil your good time thinkin' 'bout her. She'll get along jest the same's before you come, an' won't have it any harder."

" I s'pose that's so," Josiah said half to himself : " you see, I never thought there could be so much trouble in the city, where it seems as if everybody has money."

" There's a good many of 'em ain't got any, an' that's a fact. If you're so stuck on seein' Sadie agin, we'll make it our business to flash her up when there's nothin' on hand ; but as I said this mornin', she'd better stay where she is while we're busy."

Josiah realized that his friends were not at all pleased by his frequent reference to the little match-girl, and he remained silent ; but there was beginning to spring up in his mind a plan which he hoped might be carried into execution.

It is just possible that the friends of the young gentleman from Berry's Corner made a mistake in introducing him to the Brooklyn Bridge during the evening, or perhaps he was too tired to appreciate that wonderful structure; but certain it is, he did not evince the surprise or admiration which Tom and Bob had expected, and even complained of the distance, saying, after they had walked with him across and back, that he would have " liked it a good deal better if it wasn't more'n half as long."

Upon their return to Baker's Court it was not necessary for Mrs. Bartlett to urge the party to retire.

There was nothing the visitor could think of that would be so refreshing as a bed just then; and he believed no pleasure could be greater than that of being able to lie down in his own room, with the knowledge that his mother was within call, even though by such change in his surroundings his visit to the city would be materially shortened.

When Josiah awakened next morning the first thought in his mind was that of the money spent during the previous day, his second as to whether Sadie had had any breakfast, and the third, regarding the amount he would receive for the fur.

"We're goin' down to Coney Island to-day," Bob cried as his guest awakened him. "Tom an' me'll see to the tickets, an' we're countin' on the biggest kind of a time."

"But I must go up to the fur store, else I'll spend all my money, an' won't have any left to buy presents for father an' mother."

"Well, we'll do that right after breakfast," Tom replied.

An hour later the three boys left Baker's Court, Josiah carrying the fruits of his labor as a trapper closely wrapped in an old newspaper, and feeling just a trifle uneasy about entering the city shops.

It was hardly probable the establishment would be open at such an early hour; and, knowing they had plenty of time at their disposal, Tom proposed to go around Broadway to Printing House Square, where he had agreed to meet Billy Foss, who was to accompany them to Coney Island.

Master Foss was a small merchant, both in point of stature and his transactions in the newspaper line; an industrious one also, as could be told from the fact that, although intending to take a day's vacation, he was devoting the earlier hours of the morning to business.

"It's all right," he said when Tom explained that they were going up Broadway before starting on the excursion. "I wanted to sell a few papers so's all the day wouldn't be wasted, an' I'll jest about be through when you get back. Meet me down to the Herald office."

Then Tom led the way up Chatham Street, and Josiah saw the girl of whom he was at that moment thinking.

"Hello, Sadie, how's trade?" Bob shouted.

"I haven't sold a box this mornin'. It seems as if nobody needed matches; an' I reckon I'll have to go into the newspaper business, even if the boys are rough."

"Does she ever make very much?" Josiah asked in a whisper, as they were approaching the child.

"No, an' I don't know what she's goin' to do when cold weather comes. Tom an' me help her out as much as we can, an' some of the other fellers chip in a little; but it's tough for her just the same. I don't reckon she's had anything to eat this mornin', 'cause most likely Mother Hunter took all her money before she left the house."

At that moment Sadie found a customer for her

wares, and the boys walked away, Tom shouting when they were a few paces distant, that he would see her as they came back.

Josiah immediately became very thoughtful.

While sight-seeing with his two friends, he had forgotten Sadie and her troubles to a certain extent; but now, as he saw her at her work, all she had told him came into his mind, and he grew down-hearted, regardless of the fact that he was soon to see the wonders of Coney Island.

He was beginning to learn that hunger and want are frequent visitors in cities ; and as he thought of Berry's Corner, where all who were willing to work could find some way to earn sufficient money for their necessities, the metropolis lost very much of its beauty in his eyes.

On arriving at the shop a short distance above Canal Street, the boys found it open, consequently there need be no time wasted in waiting, as had been feared.

The woodchuck skins were not as valuable, in this particular dealer's estimation, as Josiah had fancied.

The merchant examined them, expressed considerable dissatisfaction at the method of curing, and ended by offering fifteen cents for each.

This was so much less than the boys expected, that they would not accept the offer, and during the next hour went from shop to shop, but without meeting any better success.

It really seemed as if every furrier in town had conspired against the trapper from Berry's Corner, and had set the price of supposedly valuable pelts at a ridiculously low figure.

"Are you goin' to sell them for that?" Bob asked when they emerged from one of the largest establishments on Broadway, where the clerks would not even examine the skins, after being told they were woodchucks.

"What else can I do?" and Josiah spoke in a mournful tone. "Father says they mustn't lay 'round the house in the winter, an' mother won't have 'em there in the summer on account of the moths, so I'd better give the whole lot away than carry 'em home again."

"Then let's go back to the first store, 'cause that man acted squarer than the rest, and didn't put on so many airs."

Josiah was greatly troubled in mind.

He had been almost recklessly extravagant since he arrived, believing the amount received from the fur would give him all the spending money needed, and with that idea had invited Sadie to accompany him to the museum on the Bowery.

Now, however, the utmost economy would be necessary, probably at the expense of the presents to his parents, and he must count carefully the pennies in order that all his hoard might not be exhausted before his father arrived.

"I have been a big fool," he said to himself: "but who would have thought things were so high in the city? Now I've got to go on with the racket even though the last cent is spent, an' I don't have anything to carry home."

By the time these mournful reflections were brought to a close they were at the shop first visited, and the trapper from Berry's Corner received the amount offered for his furs.

The sixty cents were deposited in the huge wallet, and the boys turned toward the City Hall once more. Tom urging them on at full speed in order that they might leave for Coney Island at the earliest possible moment.

But it was as if Josiah could not walk rapidly.

He paid no attention to the alluring shop windows, neither did he appear to hear what his companions said to him, until they were crossing Chambers Street, when Bob cried impatiently : —

" If you don't hurry up we won't get there till noon. So long as we've got to spend our money for it, we may as well scoop in the whole show."

Then it was Josiah suddenly awakened to the fact that his companions were urging him to greater speed ; and he said abruptly. as he halted and seized both boys by the arms to insure attention : —

" See here, fellers, it'll cost considerable money to go there, won't it ? "

" Bob an' I've 'greed to pay for everything. " We've been savin' up to give you a good time, an' it'll be done in style."

" Hold on a minute," and Josiah spoke hurriedly, as if almost ashamed of what he was about to say. " I'd like to see the place. 'cause I want to know how the ocean looks : but when I think of that little match-girl without anybody to help her, it don't seem's if it was right to spend so much money jest for fun."

" Do you mean to say we oughter give it to her?"
Tom asked in surprise.

"It would do more good than for us to spend it
havin' a swell time."

" You wouldn't have much money if you staid
'round here givin' it to every feller that was hard
up." Tom replied quite sharply. " There's more'n
a hundred jest as bad off as she is, an' we can't help
'em all. Both of us give her a few pennies when
we've had a good day's work ; but sometimes it's
tough scrapin' to get enough for ourselves."

" Now don't spoil all our fun," Bob added.
" You've come down where you never was before,
an' we wanter kind of square up for the good time
out to the farm; but how are we goin' to do it if
you get soft on everybody what's in trouble? Let's
go to Coney Island now, an' to-morrow, if you say
so, we'll give her a nickle apiece."

Josiah realized that he ought not interfere with
the plans of his friends, neither was it for him
to say whether they should devote their money to
almsgiving, and he replied : —

" I'll tell you what I wish you'd let me do: I
haven't got a great deal of spare cash ; but I'd like

to take her with us, an' am willin' to pay all she costs. It'll be a big thing for her, an' won't spoil our fun."

Tom and Bob hesitated, because they were just a trifle uncertain as to how Master Foss might fancy this unexpected addition to the party; and Josiah continued, in order to make his meaning more plain : —

"If she goes, I want to be sure an' pay her bills, an' I'll see that she ain't in you fellers' way."

"Well, s'pose we try it?" Bob said to Tom after a short pause. "It won't do any harm; an' if it's goin' to give him a better time, why we oughter let her come."

"All right; you go after her with him, an' I'll snoop down to the Herald office so's to kind of break it gently to Bill. It might not do to flash the thing too sudden on him, 'cause he never did think much of girls."

Tom hurried away as he ceased speaking, while Josiah and Bob continued on to Chatham Square, where they plunged Sadie into a state of bewilderment and amazement, by inviting her to spend the entire day at Coney Island.

"Do you think I look fit?" she asked anxiously.

"Course you do," Josiah replied promptly; "besides, nobody's goin' to see you."

This was sufficient for the child; and, stopping only long enough to deposit her tray of matches with the friendly shopkeeper, she joined the boys, Josiah feeling fully repaid for the money he was about to spend, by the look of gratitude which lighted up the pale face.

CHAPTER IX.

THE EXCURSION.

Tom was overtaken before he had walked very far; and although he and Bob had consented to Josiah's inviting Sadie to accompany them on the excursion, neither felt that it was exactly the proper thing for them to have "a girl taggin' on behind," as some of their acquaintances afterwards described it.

They would have been glad for Sadie to enjoy herself in some other direction than with them; and during the journey to the Herald office, where Master Foss was to be met, the newsdealers kept considerably in advance of their guest and the match-girl, as if not willing to admit that the two were a portion of their party.

" I expect the fellows will jest 'bout guy the life out of us for takin' her along," Bob whispered to

Tom; "but I didn't see any other way after Josiah was so set upon her goin'."

"Never mind what they say, so long's we've got her," Tom replied; "but I think we oughter put our foot down against her comin' in the first place, 'cause she's goin' to break the fun all up before night, an' I don't feel like puttin' out good money without gettin' somethin' back."

There was no further opportunity to discuss the unexpected state of affairs; for at this moment Master Foss hailed them from the opposite side of the street, and, before he could cross, Sadie and Josiah had joined the party.

Bill looked first at the match-girl, and then at his friends, in an inquiring manner, and appeared so thoroughly disturbed in mind that Bob motioned him to step into an unoccupied door-way, where he whispered hoarsely : —

"We couldn't help it, Bill, for a fact. You see, Josiah's stuck on takin' her 'round 'cause he thinks she don't have many good times, an' we was bound to do as he wanted, for when we was out to his place everything we said went."

"An' is she goin' all the way with us?" Bill asked anxiously.

"That's jest the size of it."

"Well, I wish I had known it beforehand; you wouldn't have caught me givin' up a day's work for the sake of haulin' her 'round."

"Now see here." Tom said, as he approached quickly, understanding from the delay that the small newsdealer was entering his protest against this unexpected addition to the party, "there's no use kickin', an' we've got to make the best of it. Don't get on your ear 'bout a little thing like that, an' we'll have jest as good a time as we know how."

Sadie was so thoroughly delighted with the prospect of seeing Coney Island, a place of which she had heard but never visited, that she paid no attention to the delay which was caused by Master Foss; but Josiah fancied he knew why his friends remained so long in the door-way, and it disturbed him not a little that he should have been the means of marring the day's pleasure in even the slightest degree.

At the same time he would have felt uncomfortable in mind had he gone on this pleasuring alone, knowing it would afford the match-girl so much enjoyment; and he began to talk very loudly to her regarding the vehicles in the street, the pedestrians on the sidewalk, or anything which met his gaze at the instant, in order to prevent her from becoming suspicious as to the true state of affairs.

Fortunately Sadie was so excited that she would hardly have paid attention had the excursion been delayed an hour; and when the three boys finally emerged from the door-way, Bill Foss looking decidedly ill-tempered, she had no idea her coming had caused either embarrassment or ill-feeling.

"I suppose she'll have to go, now the thing's fixed," Bill had said when the interview was brought to an end; "but I won't walk along the streets with her, that's all there is about it."

"You don't have to," Bob said soothingly. "Josiah an' she can take care of themselves, an' we'll keep a little ways ahead so's nobody'll know Sadie's with us at all."

In pursuance of this plan Bill walked rapidly, and more than once before the pier was reached did it become necessary for Bob and Tom to urge their country friend to quicken his pace.

"We want to take the next boat," the latter said

impatiently, "an' you'll have time enough to look into the store windows when we get back. If you don't make him come fast, Sadie, we'll never get there."

This threat was sufficient to cause the match-girl to urge Josiah on when he was tempted to stop at any unusual display, and they had ample time in which to make arrangements for the trip on the steamer.

Bob and Tom had proposed to assume all expenses of the day's outing, and to that end the former stepped toward the ticket-office ; but Josiah objected, saying in a whisper as he forced some coins into his friend's hand : —

" I agreed to stand what Sadie cost, so you must take this."

" I sha'n't do anything of the kind. Tom an' I are treatin' this time, an' we're goin' to do it in the best shape we know how."

" But I dragged her along, an' it ain't any more'n fair I should pay for it."

" I might have let you, if you'd got anything out of the woodchuck skins ; but they went so awful cheap, I reckon you'll need all the money you've got before your father comes."

Josiah urged the acceptance of the coins; but all to no purpose, and the young gentleman from Berry's Corner felt more disturbed in mind than ever as they walked across the gang-plank, for he was aware that by his invitation the amount which Tom and Bob had laid aside for the excursion would be sensibly reduced.

The music of the Italian band, the steamer (for, with the exception of the ferry-boat, he had never been on board one before), as well as the crowds of people, soon served to drive from Josiah's mind everything save that which was passing immediately before him, and during the trip to the Island he was in a state of surprise and delight amounting almost to bewilderment.

His first sensations were of fear lest the boat, crowded to what he fancied was a dangerous extent, would sink beneath her heavy cargo; but since nothing of the kind happened immediately after leaving the dock, he recovered from his alarm, and began to think it possible she might be seaworthy, although he was confident a dozen more people would swamp her.

The different craft on the river, or lying at the

docks, the tooting of whistles, and the confusion on the decks, caused it to seem as if he was in a different world from that in which he had lived while on the farm, and more than once he whispered to Sadie : —

"I'd be willin' to go home this very minute, if mother an' father could be here long enough to see these things. I've heard 'bout vessels; but I didn't b'lieve there could be so many in the world, an' as for water, why the brook at the farm ain't anywhere !"

Bill Foss, afraid of being suspected as one of the party, remained quite a distance from the others, which forced either Tom or Bob to stay with him in order to play the part of host, therefore both of them were not near Josiah during the entire trip, as they would have preferred; but this enforced absence did not prevent him from seeing all the sights brought into view during the passage, and when they finally arrived at their destination he had a better idea of the size of New York harbor than ever before.

Once on the dock the question arose as to how to begin what Tom and Bob intended should be a "dizzy round of pleasure."

Bill was quite as much averse to being seen with
"a girl in the crowd," as while in New York; and
for a short time the hosts were sadly at a loss to
know how the entertainment could be conducted,
in order to give the proper amount of attention to
each of their guests.

Fortunately, at this moment Sadie and Josiah
were delighted by a view of the flying-horses in
full operation, and at the same instant Master Foss
was attracted by a game of ball in which the target was a negro's head; and Bob whispered: —

" Here's our chance! You get them two on the
horses, an' I'll see that Bill has a show to hit the
nigger if he can."

Neither of the hosts participated in the pleasure,
except as a spectator; but it appeared to be enjoyment enough for them, and when fifteen minutes
had passed, this portion of the programme was
brought to a close.

Bill did not succeed in striking the target; but
the exercise, together with the fact that it was
what he called " a free blow" so far as he was concerned, had put him in the best of humor, therefore, with a magnanimity which caused his friends

no slight amount of pleasure, he was willing to so far unbend his dignity as to walk not more than a few yards in advance of Sadie.

Five cents were invested in "nigger eye-balls," five more in "bolivars," and then the sight-seers promenaded the entire length of the beach, past all the booths, stopping here and there to see some free entertainment given as an attraction to a restaurant or saloon, remaining at each one until the proprietor or an employee suggested that it was time for them to be "movin', for they didn't bring any trade to the place."

This portion of the sight-seeing had occupied the remainder of the forenoon, and then came what the hosts intended should be, and Tom announced was, the "boss part of the day."

"We're goin' right in here, an' every one is to have a plate of clam chowder," he said with the air of a millionaire, if indeed millionaires indulge in clam chowder at Coney Island.

Sadie's eyes opened wide with astonishment as the daring Tom led the way into a restaurant even more magnificent than the " Jim Fisk " establishment on Chatham Street; and, halting his party in the centre of the room, he announced to one of the waiters with not so much as a tremor of his eyelids, that they had "come for a chowder."

The man looked at these intended customers a moment, as if to decide whether they had sufficient money to pay for the desired refreshments, and then motioned them to a table at the farther corner of the room, although one near the window was without an occupant.

Tom was about to obey the mute command, when Bob stopped him by saying in a hoarse whisper:—

" Look here, if we've got to pay for these chowders jest the same as anybody else. I'm goin' to set where I want to ; " and he boldly took a chair from the desired table, seating himself with the air of one who knows his rights and is determined to have them, while the others, with more or less trepidation, followed his example.

Bill Foss did his best to appear perfectly at ease, and so far succeeded that he actually took a fragment of cracker from the plate, and began eating it as if he had a perfect right to indulge his appetite in whatever manner should please him most.

Sadie and Josiah looked uncomfortable, and probably were, during the time of waiting for their refreshments.

Both sat on the edge of their chairs as if undecided whether it would be wise to occupy them in a proper manner; and each gazed at the other in fear and trembling when Bill, emboldened by his first attempt, broke off a second and larger piece of the biscuit, putting it in his mouth at imminent risk of strangling himself.

Tom, thinking of the very important portion of the feast, whispered to Bob: —

" Why didn't you ask him how much they'd charge to fill us up with chowder? "

" What would I do that for? I reckon they'll tell us when we get through eatin', an' this firm has got money enough to stand the shot, don't you be afraid of that."

It certainly seemed as if the waiter was troubled with the same misgivings as Tom; for before bringing them what had been ordered, he returned to the table and asked : —

" Do you want one check, or five, for these chowders ? "

He looked directly at Josiah as he spoke; and the boy from Berry's Corner was beginning to feel much more uncomfortable than before, when Bob said decidedly : —

"I don't know how many we want; but I'm goin' to pay for the whole crowd."

The waiter took a check from among a number of others in his apron pocket, and placed it before the generous host, as if to intimate that it would be better to settle in advance, while a look of consternation, which he tried in vain to hide, came upon Master Green's face as his eyes rested on the printed figures.

Bill leaned over in order to see more clearly, and then gave vent to a whistle of astonishment ; but Bob was determined the waiter should not think him unaccustomed to such bills, and with no little difficulty counted out the required amount.

" How much was it ? " Tom asked anxiously, when the waiter had disappeared.

" A dollar and a quarter ! "

" What ? "

" That's what I said. I tell you they oughter bring along a slat of stuff if they're goin' to charge that much for it. I was countin' on havin' a pretty swell dinner; but I guess the chowder is 'bout as far as we'll go if things keep on at this rate."

"Well, I reckon they give a good deal, an' that's why the price is so high," Bill said in a soothing tone, and once more made an attack upon the crackers. "Of course if a feller gets all he can eat, I don't know as it's very much, considerin' we're down to Coney Island."

Now Josiah was more distressed than ever, because he had added to the liabilities of his friends, and he whispered to Bob : —

"If you're runnin' short I can let you have some."

"Oh, it's all right. I'll get through. We didn't 'low to spend less'n that for dinner, so we're solid."

Then the party waited anxiously to see how much chowder they were to receive for the large amount of money expended; and when it was finally brought Bill Foss exclaimed, even before the waiter had left the table : —

" I'll tell you, fellers, this is growin' too rich for my blood! Twenty-five cents apiece for them little bowls of chowder, when I can get all I can carry away for five cents, up to the Jim Fisk saloon, kinder looks hard."

"Well, don't say anything about it now, Billy. We've got inter the scrape, an' might jest as well enjoy ourselves. There ain't much of it, I know; but perhaps it's awful nice," and Bob set a good example to his friends by attacking his portion without delay.

During the next ten minutes the pleasure-seekers did not indulge in any extended conversation.

The time was fully occupied in trying to extract the value of their money from the food before them, and they had no opportunity for anything else.

It was not until the last crumb had disappeared that Bill Foss asked, as he pushed his chair back a few inches to show that he was perfectly at ease : —

"Well, fellers, now we've filled up, whater we goin' to do ?"

"Come outside," Bob replied; and as the party gained the board-walk he added, " The rest of you stay here while I talk to Tom a minute."

"They're goin' to count up the cash." Bill Foss

whispered as the two stepped behind a candy booth, and Sadie said to Josiah :—

" I'm sorry we went in there to dinner, for the boys spent a good deal more'n they ought to."

" Now, don't you go to worryin' 'bout that. Us fellers will 'tend to the money, an' if Tom an' Bob haven't got enough I'm willin' to put out all there is in my pocket."

Then the three waited in something very nearly approaching anxious suspense to learn whether the day's pleasuring was to end with the eating of the chowder, or if there were sufficient funds at their disposal to admit of a more protracted stay.

CHAPTER X.

A DISAPPEARANCE.

Bob and Tom looked decidedly relieved when they returned from the private interview, and there was really no need of questioning them as to the state of their finances.

"It's all right," the former said in a tone of relief. "We've got our tickets home, an' sixty cents besides, so I reckon that will be enough to do up all there is here. Now go in an' have the best time you know how. What do you want to do, Josiah?"

"I'm satisfied jest to walk 'round. There's no place to go without spendin' a lot of money."

"But we're doin' the whole figger this time. Tom an' Bill an' me can come down any day, while you can't; so we've made up our minds you shall get all that's goin', an' we'll hold back."

" But I don't want to do anything of the kind," and Josiah looked distressed. " There's no need of spendin' more money, an', besides, I wouldn't go into what you fellers couldn't share."

" Don't mind 'bout us. We'll look out for ourselves. What do you want to do ? "

" Walk 'round a little while."

" I'll tell you what it is, we're goin' in swimmin'," Bill Foss said decidedly. " I made up my mind this mornin' that if I got to Coney Island the first thing I did would be to go right inter the water."

" But it costs as much as twenty-five cents apiece to get a bathin' suit," Tom suggested.

" Well, s'posen it does ? We don't want to buy any. I'm goin' jest as I am."

" You never could do that ! How would you look runnin' 'round here all wet ? "

" I wouldn't run much till I got dry. What's the matter with layin' out on the sand in the sun ? I don't wanter to put on any frills."

" What do you think of it, Josiah ? " Bob asked.

" I don't b'lieve I'd dare to go in where the waves come up so high, an' besides, I'd a good deal rather see the things 'round here."

"I'll tell you how to fix it," Tom suggested. "Of course Sadie can't go in, so what's to keep her an' Josiah from doin' whatever they wanter for half an hour? Then we'll be dried out, an' ready to chip in for what they say."

"That's the very thing!" and Josiah spoke quickly lest his companions should object to the scheme; for he understood that by inviting Sadie he had not only added to the expense, but curtailed their pleasure to a very decided degree. Since all three of the boys appeared eager for the bath, he preferred seeing the sights in company with the match-girl.

"Where'll we meet you when we get through?" Tom asked.

"We'll come right here in half an hour," and Josiah looked around to make certain of the landmarks in the vicinity.

"Don't go too far away, else you might not get back, an' we wanter take the boat mighty soon after dark," Bob said, as Bill, impatient for his bath, hurried away.

"I'll look out for that." Josiah replied confidently. "You'll see us when you're ready to leave."

The three boys walked rapidly toward the beach; and Josiah, feeling it incumbent upon himself to play the part of entertainer, led Sadie to a canvas tent, the outside of which was covered with gaudily-painted representations of improbable animals in the most glaring colors.

"Are you goin' in?" she asked, halting in front of the "band," which was represented by a hand-organ.

"Yes, we want to see everything, an' might as well begin right here."

"But it costs ten cents."

"I know it, an' s'pose we oughter wait till the other fellers are with us; but we've got to do somethin,' an' if they wanter see these things I'll buy 'em tickets when they come back," Josiah replied. "Then if it ain't good we sha'n't be losin' so much money."

Five minutes later the boy from Berry's Corner was decidedly glad he had not waited to invite his friends; for the number of curiosities on exhibition was so small as compared with those seen in the "circus" on Chatham Square, as to make a dime appear a greater extravagance than was the quarter in the purchase of a clam chowder.

"Well, they don't swindle me that way again," he said a trifle impatiently as they came out from the tent. "Why, the fellers in Berry's Corner could rig up a better show than that for ten pins, an' then not think they was doin' very much."

Sadie had nothing to say.

She was vexed because the exhibition was so much less than what it had been represented, but remained silent through fear of adding to Josiah's disappointment, and the two walked up the beach where there were very many entertaining things to be seen free of charge.

During the next half-hour the sight-seers were oblivious to the passage of time.

A kindly-disposed waiter at one of the saloons on the board-walk allowed them to remain during the performance of an alleged band of negro minstrels, without intimating that they were bringing in no custom to the establishment, and the exhibition was so thoroughly satisfactory that for a while they forgot the engagement which should have been kept some time previous.

"The fellers'll be waitin' for us, an' I expect Bill Foss is pretty nigh fussin' hisself to death 'cause we don't come," Josiah said as he led his companion away from the entrancing spot where the music had held them spellbound. " It must be 'most an hour since we left 'em."

Sadie, who depended upon her generous friend to show her the way, had given no heed to the direction in which they traveled; and now, when they wished to return, she followed Josiah readily, ignorant of the fact that he was walking directly away from the appointed place of meeting.

The young gentleman from the country believed he had a very good idea of the course which had been pursued, and, as he thought, retraced it correctly, until fifteen or twenty minutes were spent without bringing them to any familiar spot.

Then he halted in dismay, and looked around helplessly.

" We've been goin' wrong," he said in the tone of one who has made an important discovery; and Sadie replied, as if the matter was of little concern:

" Then we must go right back."

This was what Josiah most desired; but whether he would be able to do so or not, was another matter.

He could distinguish nothing to guide him on his way, and stood in painful indecision until, noticing a look of anxiety on Sadie's face, he believed it necessary to prevent her from becoming alarmed, and therefore resolved to act as if confident he knew exactly in which direction to proceed.

It would have seemed a simple matter if he had been able to inquire the way; but, not knowing where he should go until he could see the landmarks before noticed, it was impossible to tell a third party where the boys had agreed to meet him.

In addition to these troubles he was growing weary; but it was necessary to join his friends as soon as possible, and he pushed on at the best pace which he believed Sadie would be able to maintain.

Fifteen minutes more passed, and then the match-girl understood the true position of affairs.

"You don't know where to go," she said, halting and looking up into Josiah's face.

" Well I don't, an' that's a fact."

" Neither do I."

" How are we goin' to find the fellers?" and

now Josiah began to grow alarmed. "We can't go home 'cause Bob has got the tickets, 'cept I pay another fare, an' I don't wanter leave while they're huntin' for us. I expect Bill Foss is tearin' mad by this time. It must be as much as two hours since we left 'em."

"How would it do if I went one way, an' you the other?" Sadie asked.

"I reckon that would make us worse off than ever, 'cause how could we meet again? S'posen you found 'em, you wouldn't know where I was."

"Yes, that's true; but we mustn't stand here;" and this time she took the lead, Josiah following meekly behind.

If they could have arrived at the rendezvous at that very moment, they would not have found their friends.

Their hosts and Master Foss were at the appointed place very nearly in due season; and after waiting fifteen or twenty minutes, their impatience became so great that inaction was no longer possible.

"I knew jest how it would be when you brought a girl along," Bill said angrily; "they're allers

breakin' up a feller's snap, an' why she wasn't left
behind is more'n I know. If that boy from the
country is so anxious to have 'em taggin' 'round
after him, let him wait till he goes home. It costs
too much for us to come down here, an' lose the
best part of the day jest because of her."

Inasmuch as Bill had not paid or offered to pay
any portion of the expenses, it was unkind, to say
the least, for him to make this remark; but neither
Bob nor Tom appeared to take any notice of it.

Both were as eager as Bill to enjoy every moment of the visit, but did not feel that they had
any right to blame their guest for the delay.

"I s'pose there are so many things to see that
he don't know how long he's been gone," Bob suggested. "If you an' Tom wanter go off, I'll stay
here an' wait for 'em; we'll kinder split the thing
up so's you won't lose a great deal of the sport."

"There's no fun if the whole crowd ain't together," Master Foss replied with the air of one
who is determined to feel thoroughly miserable,
and he seated himself in a martyr-like fashion on
the edge of the board walk.

During the next five minutes he allowed his

friends to see how unhappy they had made him, and then began grumbling once more.

"We might jest as well go home, an' a good deal better'n to set 'round here. What fun is there in this? I'd rather be up to City Hall Park where the fellers are, an' besides, see how much money I'm losin'! All this afternoon's business gone for the sake of hangin' on to an old sidewalk down to Coney Island."

Bill continued his complaints in a similar fashion for a long while, without receiving any reply, and then Bob's patience was exhausted.

"See here," he said sharply. "Tom an' me couldn't help this, an' I don't reckon Josiah means to do anything out of the way; but if you feel bad at havin' to stay here a little while, s'pose you start off by yourself?"

"I don't wanter go without the crowd; but I'd rather be at home."

"Here's your ticket. We're bound to wait for Josiah if he don't get back till mornin', 'cause all we came here for was to give him a good time, an' I only hope he's havin' it."

"I reckon he is, an' don't care anything 'bout

what we have to do," Bill grumbled, but he did not take the proffered ticket.

" You don't s'pose he's got lost, do you ?" Tom asked, an expression of alarm coming over his face, and Bob cried as he leaped to his feet : —

" That's jest what's the matter ! They've gone off somewhere, an' don't know how to get back."

" Then we'll have a fine time huntin' for 'em all night ! I guess I'd better go home," Bill said, and without hesitation Bob handed him the ticket once more.

" There you are ! Now do as you're a mind to. We've got to hunt for Josiah. Tom, you go 'round by the water, an' I'll skin up this way."

" Where shall I meet you ? " Tom asked, as he turned to obey.

" Down by the dock. I'll go there if I find 'em, an' you must do the same."

Bill made no proposition to aid his friends ; but, with his ticket in his hand, went slowly toward the steamboat landing, his eyes fixed upon the ground, as if afraid he might see the lost ones, and thus terminate the search too soon to please him, for he

was anxious his friends should, as he expressed it,
" get enough of taggin' 'round with a girl."

Half an hour later Bob and Tom met at the pier,
but neither had seen Josiah, and both felt seriously
alarmed.

"Do you s'pose there's any chance he'll go
home?" Tom asked.

" No, I don't reckon he'd be likely to do that,
'cause I've got the tickets, an' he wouldn't wanter
put out so much money for nothin'."

" Then I'm afraid it'll be a good deal as Bill says.
We shall spend the rest of the day, an' part of the
night, huntin' for 'em."

" That won't be such an awful long while, for
it's pretty nigh dark now."

" What *are* we goin' to do?"

" There's nothin' for it except to keep right on
huntin'. But say," Bob added, as a happy thought
occurred to him, "let's tell every policeman we
meet. They'd be sure to know Josiah, he looks so
green, an' could send him down to the pier. Folks
will be goin' home mighty soon, an' when there
ain't so much of a crowd here, it'll be easier to see
him."

This plan was acted upon without delay; and in a short time every officer in the immediate vicinity of the rendezvous knew that "a feller from the country, with a girl what didn't look very scrumptious," was lost.

Not until sunset did the two searchers meet again; and, as before, there was nothing for either to report.

Josiah and Sadie had disappeared as completely as if the earth had swallowed them, so far as these two friends of theirs were concerned: and Bob said in a tone of conviction, as he wiped the perspiration from his face: —

"It's no use talkin', Tom, they must have gone home; an' the best thing we can do is to take the next boat, for Josiah is at Baker's Court by this time."

"But s'pose he isn't?"

"There ain't any s'pose 'bout it. If he'd staid we'd found him before now, an' the sooner we go, the better."

Tom made no protest, and the two went on board the steamer. leaving behind Josiah and Sadie, who were still vainly endeavoring to find the appointed place of meeting.

CHAPTER XI.

BOB'S FRIEND.

IT was while Tom and Bob were yet searching for the missing ones, that Josiah decided it would be impossible for him to walk any farther until after taking a rest.

He and Sadie had, as it appeared to them, traveled from one end of the Island to the other without seeing any buildings which looked familiar; and when the boy from the country was so weary that it seemed impossible to take another step, he seated himself on the edge of the board walk, saying mournfully : —

" It's no use, Sadie ! We'll have to give it up for a while. I never was so tired in my life, an' don't understand where Bob and Tom can be."

" They must have gone home, 'cause it wouldn't seem reasonable we'd be walkin' 'round all this time without meetin' 'em. Perhaps they think that's where we are now."

" I don't believe they'd leave us ; 'cause you see Bob knows we'd have to buy other tickets, an' his would be wasted."

" But he couldn't stay here all night."

" He'd hold out a pretty long while before he left us," Josiah said decidedly, and Sadie ceased all attempts at persuading him her opinion was correct.

" It seems to me as if it had been two days since we had that clam chowder," the boy said after a few moments of silence. " This runnin' 'round has made me hungry. S'pose we get somethin' to eat before huntin' any more ? "

" But remember how much Bob had to pay for dinner! I think after all that money has been spent, we oughter get along a good while without anything else."

" There wasn't so very much of it, except the price ; " and the thought of what he had eaten caused Josiah to grow more hungry.

There had been so many times in her life when the little match-girl was obliged to get along without either dinner or supper, that she would have been perfectly contented to wait until the boys should be found, or, in fact, dispense with a second meal entirely; but Josiah was not accustomed to anything of the kind, and it seemed a duty which must be performed, regardless of expense.

Therefore, without further argument, he led his companion to the booth where a not very cleanly looking man was dispensing sausage sandwiches.

" There ! " he said in a tone of satisfaction, " they are five cents apiece, an' this ain't any chowder business where they tuck on the price after you've ordered the stuff. Now fill right up, an' when you can't eat any more we'll start out agin."

Sadie obeyed meekly, and when each had eaten three of the sandwiches. their hunger was appeased.

" I've had all I want," Sadie said as she wiped her mouth with the sleeve of her dress, " an' they were good; but this payin' fifteen cents for three of 'em when you can get a tony dinner up to the Jim Fisk restaurant for the same money, seems like a pretty big price."

" Yes, that's so," Josiah added reflectively. " Out our way you can buy a whole pound of

sausages for ten cents. This man must be makin'
hisself rich. "

During the five minutes spent in watching the
vendor on his supposed road to wealth, Josiah
forgot that he and Sadic were lost; and then the
girl reminded him of the unpleasant fact by
saying: —

"It won't do to wait 'round here. I'm most
certain we're nowheres near the place we agreed to
meet the fellers, an' we've got to hunt pretty lively,
'cause it'll be dark in a little while."

Josiah followed without a word of remonstrance,
although he would have been willing to remain
almost anywhere rather than continue the exercise; but Sadic walked on rapidly, regardless alike
of his or her weariness of body.

When night came they were still apparently as
far from accomplishing the object of their search as
at any time previous, and now Sadic believed the
proper course was to return to New York.

Josiah would not listen to anything of the
kind.

He insisted his friends were yet on the Island,
and announced his determination of remaining all

night rather than take the chances of leaving them behind.

" What will we do when the last boat goes ? " Sadie asked anxiously.

" Perhaps we'll find the boys before then."

" But s'posen we don't ? "

" Look here, Sadie, we won't s'posen anything about it. We've got to find 'em, an' that's all there is of it; but if the last boat *should* go before either of 'em turned up, why we'd have to walk."

" I'm 'fraid you couldn't do much of that because you're so tired now ; " and Sadie ceased her efforts at persuasion, shutting her teeth hard as she thought they might possibly be forced to remain on their feet all night; but determined to say nothing more lest the boy who had been so kind should think her importunate.

From this hour until ten o'clock Josiah and his companion alternately walked and rested, and just at the moment when he was beginning to think it would be necessary to abandon the search, a stranger of about his own age halted suddenly in front of him, as he asked : —

"Say, ain't you the feller what come down from the country to see Bob Green an' Tom Bartlett?"

"Well, s'posen I am?" Josiah replied, rendered cautious by his previous unpleasant experience.

"Nothin'; I reckoned you was, but couldn't figger out where they were. Hello, Sadie!" the stranger added as the match-girl stepped forward a few paces where she could be seen. "You down here too?"

"Yes, an' we've got lost. We come with Tom an' Bob, an' Bill Foss, but now can't find any of 'em."

"How did that happen?"

"They went in bathin', you see, an' Josiah an' me was goin' to look 'round a little while. We went into a show, an' when we come out couldn't find the place where they was goin' to meet us."

"How long ago was that?"

"Jest after dinner."

"They've gone home by this time," the boy said confidently. "It ain't likely they'd wait here so late if they didn't find you, an' you'd better toddle right up to Baker's Court."

"That's jest what I told Josiah," Sadie said

earnestly; "but he seemed to think they'd stay here."

"Of course not. What you want to do is go right on board the boat."

"But Bob's got the tickets," Josiah said hesitatingly.

"Well, that can't be helped now. Haven't you enough cash for the fares?"

"Yes; but I don't believe they'd like it if so much money was wasted."

"They can't help theirselves, if you don't turn up. It ain't likely they'd think of stayin' here all night, an' you've got to hustle 'round pretty lively if you want to get away. Come on, I'm goin' up, an' after we get into town I reckon Sadie can take you to Baker's Court."

"Of course I can," the match-girl replied confidently; and Josiah, much against his will, allowed himself to be led on board the steamer, even though he believed his friends were yet searching for him on the Island.

This second sea voyage was by no means as enjoyable as the first had been.

Both Josiah and his companion were thoroughly

tired, and the latter took advantage of the opportunity to go to sleep almost immediately after boarding the steamer.

Their new acquaintance professed to have important business with some one on the lower deck, and Josiah was left to his own reflections, which were not pleasant.

This last outlay had made serious inroads upon his already sadly depleted capital, and the disagreeable thought came into his mind that it would be necessary for him to return home minus the much-desired gifts.

"Father an' mother will have to do without anything, I'm afraid. It makes me feel awful mean to go back as if I'd forgotten all about 'em while I was here," he said to himself. "I oughter sold them woodchuck skins the first thing, an' then I'd known jest how much they was worth."

These thoughts naturally led to a desire on Josiah's part to learn exactly how much cash he had; and partially turning in his seat to prevent those in the immediate vicinity from seeing his movements, he took an account of the stock on hand.

"Here's only ninety-two cents," he said, as he returned the coins to his pocket, "an' seein's how I've got to take the fellers up to that museum, it don't look as if I'd have very much left to buy things with."

This fact, together with the weariness of body caused by long searching for his friends, detracted from his pleasant memories of the forenoon; and when the boat finally arrived at the pier, Josiah actually regretted that the following day was not Saturday instead of Friday.

Sadie was not a particularly cheerful companion after having been awakened from her nap, but she was a good guide, and this was the most important of all.

Josiah followed her through the almost deserted streets, neither speaking save at rare intervals, when the country boy, despairing of ever reaching Baker's Court, would ask how much farther it was necessary to walk.

They had arrived within a block of their destination, when an outcry from the opposite side of the street caused both to halt suddenly.

"It's Bob!" Sadie said in mingled delight and

surprise, and an instant later Master Green was listening to his friend's story of the fruitless search at Coney Island.

"Tom's 'round by the pier waitin' for you. I tell you when we got back an' found you hadn't come, things looked blue. I was 'fraid you would-n't have money enough to pay for a lodgin' down there, 'cause it would cost pretty high if they charge for beds the same as they do for chowder, an' I couldn't make out how you was goin' to get along."

"I guess we'd had to stay on the board walk all night." Sadie said laughingly; "but now we've found you there's no use fussin' any more. I'll go right home, 'cause I reckon Mother Hunter 'll be pretty ugly if I don't show up soon."

"You're goin' to our house' an' stay till morn-in'," Bob said decidedly. "You haven't earned any money, an' that old woman'll jest about break you all to pieces if you don't give her a cent. I fixed it with mother, an' you can get along without a reg'lar bed."

"I guess I can," Sadie replied promptly. "It's been so long since I knew how it felt to sleep in one. that I shouldn't get on very well if I had a bed all to myself."

While the three were talking, Tom returned breathless from long running, and was on the point of announcing that their friends did not arrive on the last boat. when he caught a glimpse of those who had been lost.

" Well, I'm mighty glad to see you, an' it's too bad we was shut off so on our swell time. We counted on showin' you everything, an' hadn't more'n begun when we got separated. It was all Bill Foss's fault; he would go in swimmin'.."

"It don't make any difference," Josiah said soothingly. " I reckon Sadie an' I saw a good deal more of Coney Island than you did. It seems to me we went over every inch of the place two or three times. Is Bill ugly 'cause we got lost?"

" He's ravin' like an Injun. Anybody'd think this blow-out had cost him all the money he'd made for a week. an' he didn't spend a single cent. He was goin' on terribly the last time I saw him."

" I'm sorry." Josiah began apologetically, and Bob interrupted him impatiently: —

" Now don't feel bad 'bout a little thing like

that. If Bill don't fancy the way things was run, he needn't go agin; an' I'll bet he won't, either. He made a regl'ar pig of hisself, fussin' 'bout where he wanted to go, an' what he wanted to see. But come on! let's get up to the house as quick as we can."

" Wait a minute; I've got some news to tell you," Tom said. " What do you s'pose the fellers are goin' to do to-morrow afternoon?"

" What fellers?"

" Pretty nigh all we know. They're gettin' up a reg'lar dinner, so's to be friends with Josiah; an' I reckon they're thinkin' of visitin' out to his farm next summer."

" Where are they goin' to have it?" Bob asked excitedly.

" There's an old canal-boat over in the Erie Basin what Tim Black knows about, an' all the fellers are to buy somethin' to eat. We strike there as soon as the mornin's business is done."

" Is Sadie in the scrape?" Bob asked, thinking of the trouble caused by her participation in the excursion.

" No, of course not. You see we've got to go in

Saunder's boat, an' she couldn't do that, you know. I expect it'll be a big time, 'cordin' to the way the fellers are gettin' ready for it."

Josiah was mildly pleased with the proposition; but he was a thoughtful boy, and could not prevent himself from mentally asking what might be the result if all these young gentlemen who proposed giving a feast in his honor should visit the Shindle farm during the following summer.

Bob and Tom were not troubled by any such possibility, simply because it did not chance to come into their minds; and both were in a high state of excitement as they led the way to Baker's Court.

CHAPTER XII.

THE MUSEUM.

WHEN Josiah awakened next morning, his first thought was that his stay had nearly come to an end.

It was Friday; and on the following day his father would arrive to take him home, — a fact which gave him no slight amount of satisfaction.

His visit to the city had been very pleasant, but at the same time he was beginning to think the Shindle farm a more desirable place of residence than any he had seen since leaving Berry's Corner.

Then, again, the state of his finances was such as to render it necessary for him to return very soon, unless he was willing to remain without sufficient money to pay his share of the expenses.

The cash expended for tickets from Coney Island

had depleted his funds to an alarming and unexpected extent.

He regretted having promised Sadie she should visit the dime museum on the Bowery; but it did not seem as if he could well withdraw the invitation, once it had been given.

"It'll take all the money I've got," he said to himself, "for of course Tom an' Bob will have to go; but it's no use cryin' over spilled milk, an' I'm goin' to finish up in the right kind of style, even if I don't carry anything home to father an' mother."

Just then Bob awakened, and, as if able to read what was troubling Josiah, asked: —

"How much did you have to pay out last night to get home?"

"I don't exactly know. What's the matter?"

"We want to give it back to you, of course."

"You won't do anything of the kind. I guess I can afford to stand that much; an' I oughter paid a good deal more, after takin' Sadie, an' makin' such a crowd when she wasn't one of your friends."

"But we're goin' to give it back all the same. That was our time, an' we allow to pay the bills."

Josiah protested he would not permit them to refund a single penny of the money; but Bob insisted, and Tom, who awakened very soon after the conversation began, joined his brother merchant so emphatically in the argument, that Master Shindle could not refuse.

"Here's what it costs for two to come up from Coney Island," Bob finally said, as he dropped the amount into Josiah's hand, "and you've got to take it."

"I'll tell you how we'll fix it," Josiah replied after a short pause. "I was countin' on takin' you fellers an' Sadie up to that dime museum, an' we'll use this money for the fares."

"When are you goin'?" Tom asked.

"Any time you say."

"Then we'd better wait till near noon, 'cause they have a regular show there, an' we don't want to go in before it begins. S'posen Tom an' me go down town a while after breakfast, an' you stay with Sadie? We oughter look out for our business a little, an', besides, I'd like to hear what Bill Foss has got to say for himself this mornin'."

Josiah was perfectly willing to be left behind,

for he had traveled around the city so much that he was thoroughly tired; and as soon as breakfast had been eaten, the young merchants set out, while Josiah walked leisurely toward Mother Hunter's with the match-girl, who thought it safest to explain, as soon as possible, the cause of her absence during the previous night, lest the old woman should be angry.

On this occasion Josiah did not go into the house. Sadie believed it might be better for him to wait on the outside until she concluded the business; and on her return, after an absence of not more than five minutes, he asked: —

" What did she say? "

" Not very much; 'cause I told her I wouldn't stay with her another day when I saw she was startin' to get into a tantrum, an' that kind of stopped her. Oh, dear," she added with a long-drawn sigh, " it must be nice to have a home like real folks, same's as Tom an' Bob have got. They tell me yours beats theirs all out an' out."

" Well, I think myself it's pleasanter," Josiah replied, not wishing to say anything disparaging of his friends' home, and yet eager that the Shindle

Farm should be given all the praise it deserved. "You see, there's more room in the country, an' folks ain't packed so close together, besides, a feller can do what he wants to without bein' afraid of gettin' lost."

"I'd like to see the country once, the grass, an' the cows, an' the butter, an' milk."

"Perhaps you will, sooner'n you think for," Josiah began, and then checked himself as if suddenly remembering he was saying too much regarding that which had occupied a prominent place in his thoughts during the past two or three days.

Sadie made no attempt to do any business on this morning, explaining that she could work all the better after they had been to the museum; and the two went to Baker's Court to wait the coming of Tom and Bob.

To Sadie's delight the young gentlemen did not arrive until dinner was ready, consequently she had another "square meal," as she confidentially told Josiah.

"I didn't really mean to hang 'round for somethin' to eat," she explained; "but so long's we'd got to wait here for 'em, I was glad they staid away till noon. After you've gone home I expect there'll be a good many times when I'll remember what we ate in the restaurant down to Coney Island, which I wouldn't have got if you hadn't come to the city, an' let that stand for a meal."

" Are you goin' to sell matches all winter?"

" I'll have to; for there's nothin' else I can do."

" But you'll freeze to death on the streets when it comes cold."

" It won't be quite so bad as that, 'cause a feller can move 'round an' go into the stores once in a while, to stand over the registers till they drive you out. It's worse at night when you can't get in anywhere."

This conversation was interrupted by the young newsdealers, who insisted the party should start at once for the museum, in order to be back sufficiently early to join their business acquaintances who were to give the feast in honor of Josiah.

" Is Bill Foss goin' to be there?" Josiah asked, probably thinking that in such a case there was every chance the pleasure would be sadly curtailed.

" Yes; but you needn't fuss 'bout it," Bob replied promptly. " I reckon he's feelin' kinder 'shamed of hisself 'cause of the way he acted yesterday, an' there won't be any trouble. Bill's a decent sort of a feller; but you see it mixed him all up to have a girl along. He allers counts on goin' ahead in everything, an' was 'fraid somebody'd see him there with Sadie. He knows pretty nigh every one of the folks in this town."

"Bill wasn't scared 'bout bein' seen with me last week, when he wanted to borrow ten cents," the match-girl retorted quite sharply.

"Did you lend it to him?" Tom asked quickly.

"I didn't have it, else I should; but since I've been livin' with Mother Hunter there ain't any chance to get that much money ahead, 'cause she's allers 'round by the time I've earned a nickle. I spoke 'bout it to show he wasn't frightened of me then."

"Now don't get riled," Bob said soothingly. "You know jest as well as we do, Sadie, that a feller like Bill wouldn't want to have it told 'round the city that he'd been swellin' down to Coney Island with a girl, and I can't blame him."

"It doesn't seem to hurt Josiah very much."

"It's different with him; he don't live here."

"Then I think it would be a good idea for Bill to stop out in the country awhile," Sadie replied; and the boy from Berry's Corner, fearing lest she might lose her temper, proposed, as the best means of putting an end to the conversation, that they go to the museum at once.

Now, as a matter of fact, neither Bob nor Tom cared to be seen with Sadie, lest some of their friends should accuse them of a desire to "stick 'round where the girls were;" but they were very careful not to let her fancy that such might be the case.

Inasmuch as she and Josiah started on ahead, they could walk a short distance in the rear without seeming to belong to the party, and neither was disposed to approach too near until they had arrived at the door of the museum.

It is only proper to say, in defence of the position which the boys assumed in the matter, that they had no idea of its being unmanly to talk with the little match-girl, or to be seen in her company; but it was the fear that their brother merchants might make sport of them, which prevented the same amount of familiarity being displayed as when they were at Coney Island.

It seemed as if Sadie would never tire of hearing Josiah tell about his home in the country; and while they were walking up the Bowery, when he would much have preferred looking in at the shop windows, she was so persistent in her questions, that all his time was occupied in giving the desired information.

She knew, quite as well as did Tom and Bob, where this particular museum which they proposed to visit was located; therefore it was not necessary for the young gentlemen from Baker's Court to give any instructions as to the course which should be pursued.

"Here's the place," she said as they halted in front of a broad door-way half-filled with gaudy posters and photographs; "an' after you see this one, you won't think the other show 'mounts to very much. Bill Foss has been here more'n ten times, an' says it's perfectly gorgeous."

Josiah made haste to purchase the tickets of admission, lest he should miss some of the wonderful sights because of lack of time. and then ushered his friends into what seemed like a place of enchantment.

On entering the main hall the first object which attracted his attention was the fat lady; and he went directly up to her, regardless of what his friends were doing.

Bob and Tom had stopped to look at some of the other attractions; but Sadie kept very close to the boy from Berry's Corner, for, since through him she had enjoyed herself as never before, it was but natural she should consider him a particular friend.

"She's awful big, ain't she?" Josiah said in what he intended should be a whisper; but the lady referred to had no difficulty in hearing the words, and smiled in a fat way upon the young visitor, in token of appreciation.

"Yes she is, an' I do wonder how she can get 'round the streets. Ain't her dress perfectly splendid? Do you s'pose that lace is real gold?"

"I reckon so; folks as big as she is must make a power of money showin' theirselves."

Again the fat lady smiled, and adjusted her red-silk robe, the skirt of which came nearly to the top of a pair of silvered boots, in order that the visitors might see the fabric more clearly.

"She's bigger'n that woman down on Chatham

Square," Sadie suggested; but in this Josiah could not agree with her.

"I don't think so," he said as he viewed the mountain of flesh critically; and, from some unexplained cause, the great woman began to frown. "I oughter know somethin' 'bout such things, 'cause last fall I guessed within four pounds on the weight of Deacon Parson's hog, an' that was two pounds nearer than anybody else could come. She's a good bit smaller than that other woman."

"Little boy, are you talking about Madame Fragile, who is exhibiting on Chatham Square?" the fat lady asked, inclining her gigantic head as near Josiah as the pillow-like shoulders would permit.

The boy from Berry's Corner was so surprised at hearing her speak, that it was impossible to make any answer; and not until the question had been repeated, did even Sadie venture to reply, when she said: —

"Yes'm, I guess that's the one we mean; she's in the Palace of Wonders down there."

"Then don't make any mistake about the size, for I am nearly ten pounds heavier than she is,

and three-quarters of an inch larger around the
waist.   She isn't such a wonderful fat woman, and
it has been conceded by the best judges in the
country that I am one of the greatest marvels of
the age."

Then the lady balanced her head squarely on
her shoulders once more, gave an extra flirt to the
short skirt in order to display the embroidery to
better advantage, and Josiah was awed.

That he had incurred the anger of such an
enormous woman was very sad, or, at least, he
thought so ; and his sorrow at having ventured an
opinion was increased when he saw her talking, as
if on terms of the greatest intimacy, with the giant.

Sadie understood that her friend was ill at ease ;
and she led him to the platform occupied by the
Circassian beauty, where he soon forgot the injury
to his feelings as he gazed in wonder and surprise
at the pink eyes and white hair of the alleged
lovely " Zerlina."

This time he was careful to make his comments
in a tone so low that the object of them could not
by any possibility hear the words ; but he would
have been treated with greater consideration had

he spoken plainly, since for her he had nothing but praise.

"Say, we mustn't hang 'round here too long," Bob said decidedly, as he and Tom approached after having taken a hasty survey of all the marvels in the room, "'cause the show will begin pretty soon, an' we won't get any kind of seats if we don't hurry."

"But I haven't looked at half the things here," Josiah replied. "How'd you finish so soon?"

"Oh, we've seen sich stuff so many times that there ain't much fun in it."

"I'd rather have a good look at what's here than to see a show like you took me to the other evenin'."

"But this'll be different, 'cause there's singin' an' dancin', an' all that sort of thing."

"It'll be more'n an hour before I'd want to leave here."

"The show'll be done by that time," Bob said in a tone of disappointment.

"Why don't you two go in, an' leave Josiah an' me here?" Sadie asked. "I'll take care he ain't lost; an' if we can't get through in time to see what's on the stage, we'll meet you outside."

"That's a good idea," Tom said approvingly; "but you mustn't stay too long, 'cause the fellers'll be waitin' for us to go over to the dinner."

"We'll be through as soon as you are," the match-girl said decidedly; and, satisfied that there would be no delay, Tom and Bob hurried away.

"Now take just as much time as you want to see everything," Sadie said when the boys had left them. "They rush right through without lookin' at half the things."

"Why can't they come here after the show is over?"

"'Cause when you go down them stairs, there's no chance to get back. You see, if it wasn't so, folks could stay in here the whole day without payin' but once."

Satisfied that he would not be interrupted, Josiah enjoyed himself thoroughly, looking at the many odd things; but he took good care not to go very near the platform on which was seated the fat lady, lest she might have some more remarks to make about a boy who could not guess nearer a lady's weight than to suppose she was less of a curiosity than Madame Fragile.

He gave no heed to the flight of time; and when Sadie suggested that their friends might be waiting, he felt quite certain no more than half an hour had elapsed since Tom and Bob left them.

"I know it's been longer," the match-girl replied, "'cause the doors are open for another show, an' that wouldn't be done if the first one hadn't been finished."

"I guess it's the same crowd that was goin' in a while ago," Josiah replied carelessly; and just then it was possible to hear, above the noise of the street, a series of yells which apparently came from the foot of the staircase by which they had entered this portion of the building.

"That's them, an' they'll be awful mad if we don't go right down," Sadie whispered as she pulled her companion toward the door.

"Josiah! Josiah-ah-ah-ah!"

There was no mistaking the name, nor the voice which uttered it; and the boy from Berry's Corner made all haste to reach the street, for the call was so imperative that he felt positive some accident had befallen one of his friends.

CHAPTER XIII.

THE FEAST.

WHEN Josiah and Sadie emerged from the building, one of the *attachés* of the museum had just succeeded in driving Tom and Bob from the entrance, to the street, and was standing on the sidewalk, shaking his fist at them in a menacing manner.

"I'll break every bone in your body if you come near this place agin!" the man cried angrily; and Bob, dancing to and fro in front of him like a marionette, the wires of which have been unskilfully pulled, replied derisively: —

"Why don't you come here an' see what you can do? We've been inter your old show, an' paid our money for it like little men. Now there's a chum of ours inside, an' we're goin' to get him out if it breaks the whole thing up."

" I'll have a policeman here before you can wink."

" Go ahead an' try it! How do we know but you've got the feller shut up in a cage, an' are goin' to pass him off for a wild man?"

" I wish I had you there for about a minute and a half!" and the man made another unsuccessful effort to catch his tormentor.

"I'm all right!" Josiah cried, as he ran out on the sidewalk, fearing lest his hosts might get into serious trouble on his account.

Just at that moment Bob failed to hear or see him, because he was busily engaged trying to keep away from the angry man; and the result was that in another instant Sadie and Josiah took part in what might have been a case for the police. but for the fact that Tom chanced to recognize them.

" It's all right now, Bob!" he cried. " Come along, Josiah;" and he started down the Bowery, while the employee of the museum, satisfied that there would be no further disturbance, re-entered the building.

" What made you stay so long?" Bob asked when the four had put a safe distance between themselves and the collection of wonders.

"It didn't seem to me as if I'd been there half an hour when we heard you shoutin'."

"Well, it's all right now, I reckon; but we must get on lively, or the fellers will be tired of waitin'."

"How long had you been hollerin'?"

"Not a great while. Jest as soon as we begun, that big chump come out to drive us off; but if you hadn't showed up we'd yelled a spell longer, whether he liked it or not."

"Don't stop to chin now," Tom said impatiently. "We can't 'ford to fool 'round a great while, an' a swell dinner waitin' for us to eat it. Where's Sadie goin'?"

"I'll stop off at the old corner," the match-girl replied quickly. "I s'pose you'll pass it?"

"Yes, it's jest 'bout as near. Now keep close to us, for we don't want any more funny business of gettin' lost."

Josiah and his companion were careful to remain immediately in the rear of Bob and Tom, although at times it was necessary almost to run, so rapidly did the two merchants walk.

"I wish you was goin' with us, Sadie," the young

gentleman said, when a throng on the sidewalk forced the leaders to come to a partial halt.

"So do I; but of course there's no chance for anything of that kind. Yesterday oughter be enough to last me a year. I never had such a splendid time in all my life, even if we did get lost."

"P'rhaps you'll see a good many like that before long," Josiah replied, and then checked himself suddenly, as if he had been on the point of saying something which should be kept a secret.

"That's a big p'rhaps," Sadie said with a laugh which was very like a sob. "There ain't many in this city what think of givin' a girl like me a good time. an' you're goin' off so soon that I won't even so much as hear of dime museums or restaurants with fifteen-cent dinners."

"You mustn't go to feelin' bad, 'cause things'll come 'round right somehow."

"Of course they will, an' even if they don't, I've been to Coney Island, an' all them places, so when it ain't very jolly, I'll think of what I have had, 'an there'll be a heap of satisfaction in that."

Now the party had arrived at the corner where

Sadie spent her time trying to sell matches, and Josiah cried:—

"If we get back before dark, I'll see you to-night."

"There ain't much chance of that; but I'll be here in the mornin'."

"Come on!" Bob shouted, "I reckon them fellers are jest 'bout wild 'cause we didn't get there before."

Josiah was forced to run now in good earnest, and Sadie was left on the corner looking after them very seriously until they were lost to view in the distance.

Tom and Bob continued on at a rapid pace, slackening the speed only when it was absolutely necessary, and on arriving at the rendezvous found eight of Tom's and Bob's friends, who had been waiting with every evidence of impatience.

Bill Foss was among the number, as was very proper since he had been selected to fill the responsible position of Master of Ceremonies, and Josiah fancied his unusual show of good-humor and friendship arose from the fact that he was ashamed of his behavior on the previous day.

He greeted the country boy with a warmth which was hardly warranted in view of the fact that they had been acquainted such a short time, and introduced him in the most friendly manner to each of the young gentlemen who had done their share toward buying materials for the feast.

"Where's Saunder's boat layin'?" Bob asked, as he saw that every boy had a package under his arm, thus showing he was ready to proceed to the meeting place.

"Down here by the dock," Bill replied. "We would have had her ready before this; but Sim Jones an' his gang are 'round there, an' we didn't want 'em to see where we was goin'."

"You ain't 'fraid of them, are you?" Tom asked quickly.

"Indeed we ain't; but you see there's no need of gettin' up a row now, 'cause we haven't any more time than we want to spend in the canal-boat. I've jest come over from there, an' I'll tell you she's fixed great! We've bought a lot of candles, so needn't come back till we get ready."

At this point Jimmy Skip went out to reconnoitre, and on his return reported that Sim Jones and his friends were no longer to be seen, consequently there was nothing to cause the would-be feasters any further delay.

The boat which had been borrowed did not appear to be very staunch, and certainly was not cleanly.

She was about one-third full of water, and it was necessary this should be removed before the party went on board, otherwise the craft would have been swamped by the additional cargo, therefore, with two tomato cans as bailing dishes, Jimmy and Bill went to work.

Ten minutes later everything was ready for the departure.

Bill brought a pair of oars from its hiding-place on the dock, and the boys clambered on board with the greatest care in seating themselves that every inch of space might be economized.

The merry-makers had worked silently to prevent the possibility of being overheard by any of Sim's party, and in perfect silence they pushed out past the pier, Bob and Tom plying the oars when they were once in the stream.

It was not an eventful, but rather a long voyage

to the Erie Basin, where the craft which was to
serve as banquet-hall was lying.

Built after the fashion of other canal-boats, there
was nothing particularly prepossessing in appearance as viewed from the outside, and Josiah thought
they had taken a great amount of trouble in order to
reach an undesirable place for the festivities.

"Wait till you see the cabin," Bill said, much
as if he read by the expression on their guest's
face the misgivings in his mind. "I have fixed
her in great shape, an' after we get inside, with
the boat pulled under the pier, Sim Foss can sneak
'round all he wants to without findin' where we
are."

Josiah soon learned that at least a portion of
Bill's statement was correct, although he failed to
see any evidences of the "fixin'."

The cabin was apparently as the owners of the
boat had left it, save for four empty bottles in one
corner; and these, Master Foss explained, had been
brought to serve as candlesticks.

That they would be free from the scrutiny of any
one who chanced to pass that way seemed positive, when the hatch was drawn, and the interior
of the stuffy cabin shrouded in darkness.

Jimmy took from his pocket a fragment of candle, and lighting it, placed it in one of the bottles, after which he awaited the coming of Bill. who had remained behind in order to hide the boat from view.

Josiah seated himself on the locker which ran across one end of the tiny apartment. and looked around wondering how the arrangements for any very elaborate feast could be made in that place.

It did not seem to him that the cabin was as appropriate an apartment for a gathering such as it was intended this should be. as many others which might have been selected.

The odor of bilge-water from the hold; the dust which covered every portion of the wood-work to the depth of at least half an inch; and the general air of decay everywhere apparent, caused him to feel gloomy rather than happy.

The remainder of the party, however, were not troubled with any such sentiments.

According to their ideas this was the jolliest kind of a place in which to spend a few hours. and Jimmy Skip regretted that the scheme had not been devised sufficiently early to admit of their making arrangements to remain at least one night in such a snug hiding-place.

"We could have done it jest as easy as not," he said, "if we'd started in yesterday mornin'. Then when you fellers got back from Coney Island you mighter come right here. an' we'd had supper ready. I wonder if your father wouldn't stay over a day, Josiah, so's to give us a chance of tryin' the snap?"

"I don't believe he would," was the prompt reply, for Master Shindle had no desire to remain where he was any longer than should be absolutely necessary.

At the expiration of ten minutes Bill Foss returned, and announced with the air of one who brings important news : —

"I've got the boat now where she can't be seen, no matter how many people are foolin' 'round, an' do you know I believe Sim an' his gang are jest comin' across ! There's a crowd leavin' Pier Eight, an' I'll bet it's them."

"Well. let 'em come." Bob said carelessly. "If you've hid our boat, they won't make much by snoopin' round here ; an' we've only got to keep still so's folks can't hear us. Now, what are you goin' to do with the things?"

"The stuff to eat, do you mean?"

"Yes; where you goin' to put it?"

"Right over where Josiah's settin'. We can spread all the papers down, an' they'll be jest as good as a table-cloth. Now come on, fellers, let's see what you've brought;" and Billy proceeded to further illuminate the cabin by placing a lighted candle in the neck of each of the remaining bottles.

In a very few moments the delicacies were spread on the locker, ready for the feasters to begin operations.

There was no reason to complain of lack of quantity or variety.

Jimmy Skip had brought two pounds of bologna, cut in substantial slices; Bill Foss, in addition to the candles, contributed a large number of crullers and a quart of peanuts; Tim Murray added to the collection three dozen pickled sheep's tongues; and, by consulting with his friends, each fellow had been able to secure some dainty different from the others, therefore the assortment was as great as there were members of the party.

"It looks as if you fellers was feelin' pretty hungry," Josiah said, as he surveyed the ample supply of food.

"We didn't have any dinner to-day, you see, 'cause we was kinder waitin' for this thing; an' I reckon that stuff'll look sick by the time we get through with it," Bill said, as he began to arrange the eatables in what he intended should be a most appetizing manner.

He had hardly commenced his work when a noise was heard from the deck, as if several persons had leaped suddenly down from the pier; and the would-be feasters looked at each other in surprise, not unmixed with alarm.

"We've got to keep mighty still," Bill whispered, "'cause somebody's down here, an' we must find out who it is."

"But s'posen they're gettin' ready to haul the boat away?" Tom suggested in the same cautious tone. "We should be in a fine fix if we got towed up the river ten or fifteen miles, wouldn't we?"

This was a contingency for which Master Foss had made no provision; and as the possibility of such a change of location presented itself, he in turn began to grow alarmed.

"We'll have to find out who's there." he said. after a brief pause. "You fellers keep quiet, an' I'll see if I can peek through the cracks in the hatch."

Bill soon learned that this was an impossibility ; and, since the noise was not repeated, he believed it safe to venture out.

"There isn't anybody up here," he said, after gazing around an instant.

"They must be out on the dock : you wanter look careful, 'cause if Sim Jones's crowd should be anywhere 'round they might make trouble."

As Bob spoke he ascended the companion-way. followed by the others; and during ten minutes the feasters remained on deck, while Bill and Jimmy scoured the immediate vicinity in a fruitless search for possible mischief-makers.

While the investigation was being made on shore, every one was so intent on satisfying himself the work was done in a thorough manner, that no attention was paid to a slight noise from the cabin, as if the stern windows had been raised.

Therefore it was without question of any mischief having been done, that Bill led the way below once more, convinced they were in no danger of an interruption.

Hardly had he gained the cabin when a cry of dismay burst from his lips; and, as if unable to speak, he stood pointing toward the locker, on which, but a few moments previous, had been placed the materials for the proposed dinner.

" Where's the stuff gone? " Bob cried in astonishment, pressing forward as if thinking the wrappings, which was all that had been left behind, might give some clew to the whereabouts of the provisions.

" What's the matter? " Josiah asked from the top of the companion-way, it not having yet been possible for him to descend because of the crowd at the foot of the stairs.

" Matter! " Bob wailed: " why, somebody's gone an' stole everything while we was on deck; an' how they coulder got away is what puzzles me! There ain't so much as a single peanut left! "

Josiah was so unnerved by the sad tidings that in attempting to descend he fell the entire length of the stairs; and when the confusion attendant upon the accident had subsided, the boys began a thorough search for the missing dainties.

"While we were on deck somebody crawled through that window." Tom said, as he pointed to the footprints which could be seen in the dust from the ledge to the locker.

"It's Sim Jones, that's who it is!" Bill cried. as he ran on deck : and an instant later his suspicions were verified by seeing the young gentleman in question, together with four of his friends, rowing hurriedly out of the basin.

CHAPTER XIV.

THE PURSUIT.

THE first impulse of the angry givers of the feast was to start in pursuit of the thieves; and Bill Foss had begun to clamber out on the dock in order to get the boat, when Bob stopped him by saying : —

" Hold on! It's no use to do that! We couldn't catch 'em now with only one pair of oars, for they've got too much of a start. The best way will be to lay for 'em to-night over on the other side."

" But they've stole all our grub!" Bill replied angrily as he halted, "an' if we wait two or three hours there'll never be a chance of gettin' it back."

" 'There's no show of catchin' them anyhow, so what's the use of pullin' all 'round the river for nothin'?

By this time Bill began to realize that pursuit would be useless, and he came back to where his companions were standing as if dazed by the bold outrage.

"I knew it was Sim Jones gettin' into that boat on the other side jest before I came below: but what beats me is, how he found out where we was? He must have follered me this afternoon."

"I don't reckon there was any need of that," Tom added. "They could see us all the time while we were comin' over, an' after you got inside I reckon they rowed mighty hard. It wouldn't be a great job to sneak up under the stern of this boat, an' then, while one of the fellers made a noise on deck, the others crawled in through the windows. That's the way of it."

There was but little satisfaction in thus settling the method of the robbery; and Bill asked impatiently as he looked at each of his friends in turn: —

"What'er we goin' to do 'bout it? Seems pretty tough to let them fellers break our good time up when we've counted on stayin' here all the afternoon an' evenin'. There won't be any fun loafin' 'round with nothin' to eat."

" S'posen all hands of us go ashore an' buy somethin' more ?" Jimmy suggested. " We ain't got
the cash to get so much as we had before : but what
we can scare up'll be better'n nothin'."

Bob and Tom looked at each other in dismay.

They had spent all their surplus money on the
trip to Coney Island, and had no more than enough
to buy their supply of papers when Josiah's visit
should have come to an end and they resumed
work once more.

Therefore it was impossible for them to act upon
Jimmy's suggestion, and at the same time they
felt decidedly awkward in refusing.

It seemed as if Master Skip could read their
thoughts, for he added almost immediately : —

" We don't expect you two fellers to buy anything. We started to get up a reg'lar dinner here,
an' are goin' to do it ourselves, or go without any."

" Bob an' I would like to chip in our share if we
had the cash : but we was flyin' kinder high yesterday, an' are mighty nigh broke now."

This remark served as a reminder to Bill Foss
that he accepted the hospitality of these two on
the previous day, and at the same time had acted

decidedly disagreeable. Therefore, in order to make amends, he very quickly adopted Jimmy's plan.

"Come along," he said as he clambered on the dock once more. "If we're goin' to do the thing there's no use foolin' 'round, an' after we've had our time out, all hands of us'll go for Sim Jones an' his crowd."

The other subscribers to the feast followed him without delay, and the young gentlemen from Baker's Court were left to "keep ship" until their companions returned.

"It's kinder tough for them to put out all the money," Tom said reflectively; "but I don't see how we can help it."

"I mighter done my share," Josiah replied thoughtfully; "but I wanted to save what I had to get presents for father an' mother, an' I'd rather do that than have anything to eat."

"There's no use talkin' about it," Tom said, more than willing to put the very unpleasant subject from his mind. "If them fellers invited us here, it was 'cause they wanted us, an' now they can go ahead an' do as they please. Some other

time we'll get even with 'em. I wish I'd thumped
Sim Jones when I had a chance this mornin'. It
seemed to me that I oughter done it."

"Why, what was he doin'?" Josiah asked.

"Nothin', only kinder lookin' as if he was tryin'
some mischief. He acted too sweet, that's what's
the matter with him; an' when Sim gets on such a
face you wanter watch out for him."

"Do you s'pose the other fellers will catch
him?" Josiah asked.

"Course they will! I'd agree to set up all night
rather'n lose the chance of payin' him off for what
he's done," and Bob shook his fist in impotent
rage toward that point where the thieves had last
been seen.

Then the hosts returned, each carrying a parcel,
and once more the locker was covered with a
varied collection of dainties.

"There!" Bill said, when he had arranged the
provision on the impromptu table to his entire satisfaction. "We won't leave this place agin with so
much stuff spread out, if every feller in Jersey
jumps on the deck. They sha'n't fool us twice in
the same way. I reckon Sim was mad 'cause we

didn't invite him to chip in with us, an' that's why he got away with the dinner."

There was no delay in beginning the feast after it had been made ready.

Bill invited the guests to commence, by saying, with a majestic wave of his hand toward the locker: —

"Pitch right in, fellers, an' fill yourselves up. This ain't no twenty-five cent chowder at Coney Island; but I'll bet you'll feel a good deal better when you get through with it than we did down there yesterday."

During the next fifteen minutes but little conversation was indulged in, for every boy seemed to think it his solemn duty to eat as fast and as much as possible.

Josiah was the first to retire from what seemed very like a contest, and then one by one the others fell out until the feast had come to an end.

Bill added to the illumination of the cabin by lighting the entire stock of candles, and then, as a fitting finale to the festival, produced a package of cigarettes.

"Don't you smoke?" he asked, as Josiah refused the proffered tobacco.

"I promised mother I wouldn't, so you see I can't," the boy from Berry's Corner replied, and the other guests looked at each other as if they thought there was something comical in the reply; but no one ventured to laugh.

Josiah was the only member of the party who did not indulge in smoking; and the result was that in a short time the cabin, closed as it had been to prevent intrusion, was filled with the pungent odor, greatly to the annoyance of the boy from the country.

He did his best to hold out against the noisome vapor, lest by making a complaint he should bring the party, arranged in his honor, to an untimely end; but when the hosts lighted their second supply of cigarettes, it was impossible for him to remain silent.

"I guess while you fellers are smokin' I'll go up on deck, an' look 'round. I never saw a canal-boat before, an' this is a good chance."

"Don't feel sick, do you?" Tom asked solicitously.

"No, not exactly; but I'd rather go up-stairs."

"Too much smoke here, that's what's the matter," Bill Foss said pityingly, as if pained because the boy for whom the feast had been particularly prepared was not sufficiently hearty to indulge in the alleged pleasures of men of the world like himself.

Josiah did not venture into the cabin again. but, after filling his lungs with fresh air, seated himself at the head of the stairs where he could hear what was being said by his friends below, and also take part in the conversation.

It seemed to him a very long while before the young gentlemen were willing to leave the scene of the festivities; and they might have remained much longer, to his discomfort and disquietude, had there been a larger stock of cigarettes on hand.

As it was, however, when the tobacco was exhausted, the cabin of the craft had no further attraction for the merry-makers; and Bill said as he rose to his feet: —

"Come on, fellers, we might as well start for Sim Jones now. It won't do to wait too long, for fear he'll sneak off home."

The chase for the boy who had robbed them offered quite as many inducements in the way of pleasure as an additional supply of cigarettes would have done, therefore no objection was made to the proposition; and, five minutes later, all the party were on board the leaking boat, pulling rapidly toward the New York side of the river, leaving behind them only the fragments of candle and the offensive odor of tobacco.

As a starting-point for the search, it was decided to go directly to the pier from which Bill believed he had seen Sim leave for the Jersey shore; and there was found the boat in which he had probably rowed across to the basin, but with her ended all clew to the direction taken by the thieves.

Master Foss was too good a general to allow anything of this kind to distress him. In fact, he rather prided himself on his abilities as an amateur detective, and lost no time in making what he believed to be a proper disposal of his party.

Two of the boys were sent toward the Battery, two more in the opposite direction, and the remainder ordered to proceed toward City Hall Square.

Bill's instructions to his subordinates could hardly be mistaken, so simple and expressive were they.

"Keep right on huntin' till you find 'em. an' then come down to Dick Murray's stand where I'll be waitin'. Don't let them know you wanter get hold of 'em; but scoot back so's all hands of us can do the rest of the job. We need the whole crowd, 'cause there ain't less'n five in their gang."

Being unacquainted with the city. Josiah was allowed to remain with the leader of the forces: and when the scouts had set out, Bill conducted the boy from Berry's Corner to the rendezvous.

Dick Murray, who had arrived at the dignity of owning a newstand only a few months previous. was a friend of all those who were so eagerly searching for Sim Jones, and at once made the new-comers welcome by inviting them into the tiny apartment which he occupied during very cold weather.

"Sim Jones is goin' to get hisself inter trouble some of these fine days," Dick said, shaking his head sagely. "That feller's actin' altogether too smart."

"In case we catch him to-night, he'll be in trouble mighty soon," Bill replied with a show of anger. "If he thinks he can steal things the way he did this afternoon, an' then get off without a thump, he's mistaken. I ain't got much time to hunt 'round for sich as him: but I sha'n't go to sellin' papers agin till this thing is squared."

"The trouble is, Bill, he's got his gang with him, an' you know it won't do to have a row on the street, 'cause you wouldn't wanter get locked up."

"I'd like to see the cop what could catch me, if I knew he was comin'," Master Foss replied.

Then he proceeded to tell a long yarn about an encounter he once had with some newsboys from Brooklyn, which was interrupted by the police, when only his legs saved him from arrest.

By the time this story, in which Master Foss posed as a hero of the first water, was concluded, Tom arrived, breathless from rapid running.

"All that crowd are down by the Vesey Street Market now, an' they've got a good deal of the stuff with 'em. If our fellers would only come in this minute, it wouldn't take us a great while to clean out the whole gang."

Bill was immediately plunged into a state of the greatest excitement, and but for the fact that Sim's party numbered five, he would have insisted on making the captures single-handed.

" We'll have to wait, I reckon." he said with a sigh. " an' it'll be jest our luck to find 'em gone when we get there."

If " luck " had any part in this evening's doings, then it certainly favored Master Foss; for in less than five minutes from the time Tom arrived, every member of the party returned to report his inability to find the boy who had attempted to destroy their pleasure.

Bill did not wait to give the new-comers any particulars regarding the information brought by Tom; but simply commanded them to " foller the best they knew how," and set off at a rapid pace with Tom and Josiah by his side.

Upon reaching a point a short distance from where the evil-disposed crowd was supposed to be, the leader of the force halted, and thus mapped out the plan of battle : —

" We'll sneak right up on 'em, so's they won't hear a thing. an' then make a rush. I'd like to tie their hands. an' leave 'em on the sidewalk till most mornin'. I reckon that would serve 'em out for stealin' the grub. Now come on ! "

The attack was successful so far as surprising the enemy was concerned, but the captures were not made as readily as Bill had fancied.

Sim and his friends, knowing full well the possibility of pursuit and an attempt at punishment, were prepared for just such an onslaught; and the result was that instantly Bill's force appeared, each of the plunderers was ready to defend himself to the utmost.

As a matter of course, a pitched and exciting battle ensued.

Josiah, to whom no orders had been given, save in a general way when Master Foss instructed all the party on their duties, felt it incumbent upon himself to assist his friends, and the first blow had hardly been delivered when he was in the thickest of the fray, receiving more in the way of punishment than it was possible for him to return.

It appeared as if Sim and his friends had some especial cause for complaint against this boy from the country, and were doing their utmost to pummel him, while they paid but little attention to the others.

It was just at the moment when Josiah began

to realize he had placed himself in a very awkward position, that the fight was stopped as if by magic, at the cry : —

" Cops ! Cops ! "

It was Jimmy Skip who gave the alarm ; being too small to make much of a show as a belligerent, he had assumed the part of sentinel to guard against just such a danger.

" Come on ! " Tom shouted ; and Josiah, not a little bewildered by the suddenness with which his friends departed, each in a different direction, stood motionless, unable to so much as take a single step.

He heard Tom and Bob shouting from a distance, and yet paid no attention to anything until a heavy hand was laid upon his shoulder, and, looking around quickly, discovered that he was in the clutch of a burly policeman who appeared far from friendly.

CHAPTER XV.

THE ARREST.

JOSIAH'S bewilderment was soon turned to alarm.

Although never having been in the city before, he understood thoroughly well that he was under arrest: and the idea of being taken to jail was to him something so terrible, that he trembled as if with an ague fit.

"Why is it you little rascals can't get along without fighting?" the officer asked, shaking the boy from Berry's Corner, as if to render his words more emphatic.

"I didn't mean to fight: leastways it didn't seem as though I was doin' it, till all the crowd got together," Josiah replied in a tremulous tone.

"Oh, you didn't, eh? I s'pose you wanter make out that somebody wound you up, and you couldn't help yourself? I've had my eye on you, young feller, for a good many weeks, and don't believe you'll trouble me any more."

"It couldn't have been so long as that," Josiah replied almost boldly, now that his presence of mind was returning. "I didn't get inter the city till last Monday, so I reckon you must have made a mistake. Besides, I'm goin' home to-morrow."

"I hardly believe you will. If you don't get a chance in the Reformatory this time, it'll be odd. You can't play off that old dodge 'bout not livin' in the city, with me; I've known you too long."

" But it's the truth, all the same:" and fancying he was mistaken for some other boy, Josiah's alarm increased once more.

The word "reformatory" had an ugly sound to him; and instantly it had been uttered there came into his mind a picture of a horrible dungeon which he, loaded with chains, would occupy for an indefinite time.

Even had he been disposed to say anything more, there was no opportunity for him to do so.

The man pulled him roughly along by the coat collar in such a manner as to cause him consider-

able discomfort and no little pain, and he felt that it would be many weeks, perhaps years, before he again saw Berry's Corner.

The officer and his prisoner had hardly got a dozen yards from the battle-field when Josiah's friends came in sight, taking good care, however, to remain at a respectful distance from the policeman, who made several attempts as if to capture them.

"Don't be afraid, we'll see you out of the scrape," Josiah heard Bob cry; and from that time until they reached the station-house, he was followed by similar injunctions from different members of the party, each of whom seemed to consider the words necessary, in order that the prisoner might not lose courage.

Nothing short of absolute liberty could have revived Master Shindle's spirits while he was in the embrace of the strong arm of the law.

Although both Tom and Bob assured him they would "see him through all right," he had a clear idea that their influence must be very slight in the premises.

At the entrance to the station-house, Bob motioned for his friends to halt as the prisoner and his captor disappeared behind the heavy door, and then said in a low but earnest tone : —

"See here, fellers, it won't do to let Josiah stay there, even if all of us has to go down to the Island for a month. His father would be pretty nigh crazy if he knew his son was arrested, an' we've got to get him out somehow."

" How you goin' to do it? " Tom asked anxiously.

"S'posen we wait till that cop comes out, an' then all hands sneak in and tell the officer in charge jest how it happened? If we agree to take Josiah's place, he oughter let him go."

" What do you wait till the policeman leaves for? Why wouldn't it be better to do the talkin' now? "

" 'Cause that feller's down on the boys what hang 'round the market, an' jest as like's not he'd take us all in."

It was not necessary they should wait very long for the officer. He had made the charge, and then, his responsibility having ceased, was returning to his beat as soon as possible.

The boys were careful not to impede his progress, and when he emerged from the station-house they were hidden from view : but three minutes later. when the sound of his retreating footsteps told that he had turned the corner, all re-appeared once more, ready to rescue their unfortunate companion, if it could be done with no other weapons than their tongues.

Master Foss did not attempt to longer act the part of leader.

The situation was so grave that he understood he was not competent to deal with it in a proper manner, and to Bob was given the management of the entire affair.

Master Green entered the station-house, his friends following close behind, with a more subdued air than he had worn when explaining what might be done. The very atmosphere of the place seemed to oppress him, and it was an exceedingly humble boy who presented himself to the sergeant at the desk. trying to render his voice steady as he said hesitatingly : —

" Look here, Mister, that cop just brought in a feller from the country what wasn't doin' any harm, an' we've come to see if we can't get him out."

"Oh, wasn't doin' any harm, eh? The officer brought him here just because of that?"

"That's the truth of it," Bob replied firmly. "Us fellers got into a row with Sim Jones' crowd 'cause they stole our grub, an' Josiah was along, so he pitched in, of course. It wasn't his fight; but he was helpin' his friends, do you see?"

"Yes, I see. He was fighting, and so were you, according to your story."

"That's it, that's jest it," Bob said eagerly; and now Tom came forward by his partner's side, as if thinking it might strengthen the cause. "We're the ones what made all the trouble, an' you oughter 'rest us instead of him. Why, look here, Mister, that feller's father's comin' here to-morrow mornin' to take him home, an' what kind of a scrape will the old man be in when he finds his boy locked up in jail?"

"His boy should avoid making trouble for his father, by not fighting."

"I've jest told you it didn't happen that way. We started the row, an' I s'pose he couldn't help hisself, so he got into the fuss. You see, he didn't seem to know what was meant when we hollered 'cops!'; but stood still like a chump till the officer had him by the back of the neck. If he'd belonged in the city, that big feller never'd caught him; but he was green, an' now we want you to let him go."

It was evident the sergeant was interested; but whether because of Josiah's unfortunate position, or the earnestness of the boy before him, it would have been difficult to say.

At all events, instead of dismissing the young pleader, as probably would have been done under other circumstances, he condescended to argue with him.

" Do you think when an arrest has been made that we can let the prisoner go, or keep him here, just as we please?"

" What's to hinder?"

" The station-house is only intended for the reception of prisoners during the night, until they can be taken to court; and when a person is committed, it is necessary for us to show him up in the morning, or get ourselves into trouble."

" But what's the sense of keepin' Josiah when he oughter go home?"

" Because we must have a prisoner to answer to his name."

" Then we can fix that easy enough," and Bob looked decidedly relieved. " You let him go, an' I'll go back in his place. When I come inter court termorrer mornin', it'll take more'n one cop to find out my name ain't Josiah Shindle."

" In other words, you want me to assist in the escape of a prisoner ? "

" No, I don't. Jest make a swap, that's all. What's the sense of sendin' a boy like him down to the Island ? He's so green he couldn't do anything; but they'd get a pile of work outer me, an' it would be better all 'round. Besides, if one ain't enough, the whole of us'll go in, won't we, fellers ? "

At this appeal, the entire party ranged themselves in front of the sergeant.

Then each in turn announced his willingness to submit to imprisonment for any indefinite period, provided the boy from Berry's Corner was allowed to go free.

The sergeant looked at them scrutinizingly, and called for the turnkey, saying as that functionary appeared : —

"You can lock these boys up, and let the youngster you just carried down-stairs go. They want to make a swap. It seems to be a good trade when we're getting ten for one."

The turnkey did not appear to understand the matter, and while he stood in the door-way hesitatingly, Josiah's substitutes marched boldly toward him.

Before they reached the door, however, the sergeant called them back, and asked his subordinate : —

"Did you lock that boy up who was brought in a few moments ago?"

"Not yet, sir. Your orders were to let him run loose."

"Very well. Bring him here. I didn't enter his name on the books, so I don't fancy there'll be any trouble in making the exchange for which these young gentlemen are so anxious."

A few moments later Josiah, looking very pale and thoroughly frightened, was ushered into the room.

A cry of surprise and joy burst from his lips as he saw his friends.

"You can take him away with you," the sergeant said, "and I don't fancy it will be necessary for any of the party to stay in his place; but remember this: If either of you are brought here within the next six months on a charge of fighting, I shall do all I can to have it go hard with the offender. I want you to promise to keep away from the Vesey Street Market, unless it should be necessary to visit that place on business."

It can readily be understood how gladly Josiah's friends promised to do as the officer wished, and in the shortest possible time afterward they took their departure, each mentally congratulating himself that he was not to spend the night in a cell in the station-house.

"Now, that's what I call doin' the thing in great shape," Bill Foss said when they were on the sidewalk once more. "It looked one time as if Josiah was goin' to see more of New York than he wanted."

"I guess it would jest about have killed father if he'd found me in jail when he came," the boy from the country said half to himself; "an' I'm glad he'll be here to-morrow mornin', cause I've got all the city I need."

" Now, don't let a little thing like that trouble you," Bob said soothingly. "It doesn't 'mount to anything."

" But I reckon it would if it hadn't been for you," Bill Foss replied emphatically.

" I didn't cut much of a figger in it, an' if I did, it wasn't any more'n Josiah would 'a done for me; so what's the use of makin' all this talk?"

Then Bob changed the conversation by asking if any of the party had noticed in which direction Sim and his friends fled; and in a few moments all, with the exception of Josiah, were deeply engaged discussing the probability of their being able, at some future time, to mete out the proper amount of punishment to those who attempted to destroy the pleasure of the afternoon.

Josiah took no part in the conversation because of his mental troubles. Although he had escaped from a prison cell so readily, he was fully alive to the fact of what his fate might have been but for his friends; and it seemed now as if he was in danger of being re-arrested every moment he remained in the city, until the arrival of his father.

It is more than probable he would have returned home without waiting for the morning, had such a thing been possible ; but since that could not be, the only place of refuge was Baker's Court, which point he wished to gain at the earliest convenient hour.

So impatient was he that it seemed a long while before his friends were ready to separate for the night; and once alone with Tom and Bob, he urged them to make all speed toward the court.

"Why, it looks like as if you was still 'fraid of bein' 'rested," Tom said laughingly.

"Well, I am," was the candid reply. "You see, I never thought anything like that could happen, an' now I've had such good proof, it don't seem safe to stay out on the street. Besides, I'm tired, an' the sooner we go back the sooner we'll get to bed."

Bob and Tom did not delay after understanding how their friend felt; and, half an hour later, the three were in the tiny chamber at Baker's Court, Josiah congratulating himself over and over again upon the fact that this was the last night he would be obliged to remain in the city.

CHAPTER XVI.

THE COUPON.

MRS. BARTLETT had not yet called the boys to breakfast, when Master Foss and his companions of the previous day arrived at the court to escort Josiah to the ferry where he was to meet his father.

"You see, I was 'fraid you fellers might take Josiah off where we couldn't find you, if we waited much longer," Bill said when Tom explained why he could not invite the party into the house.

"But he ain't thinkin' of goin' home till night," Master Bartlett replied in surprise.

"I know that; but we wanter go down to the ferry with him. You know a lot of us are countin' on visitin' his farm next summer, an' it won't do any harm if we see the old man."

"But look here, Bill, you mustn't foller us

'round all day, for I don't b'lieve Mr. Shindle would like it."

" Oh, we don't 'low to do that. Jest wanter get 'quainted with the farmer. We'll take a sneak when you come 'cross the ferry."

" All right. Wait here, an' as soon's breakfast is over we'll be down."

Then Tom re-entered the house without telling Josiah of the escort which had arrived.

The boy from Berry's Corner was deeply engaged in packing the well-worn valise, and counting his money in order to see how much he might spend in purchasing the presents for his father and mother.

He was happier now than he had been on the Monday morning previous; for, although charmed to a certain degree with the city, he preferred to live in the country, and was decidedly impatient to be at Berry's Corner again, where there would be no danger of another arrest.

Life in New York no longer had any charms for him. He had seen Bob and Tom at work, and felt certain that next summer when called upon to weed the long rows of carrots, the task would seem less laborious as compared with theirs, and decidedly more pleasant.

The city was so big, the throngs of people on the street so intent on their own business without apparently being able to bestow a thought upon others, and the noise so wearying and bewildering, that it would be very pleasant to stand once more by the side of the long, dusty road which stretched away in the distance, like a yellow ribbon between the green and nodding trees.

Fishing for chubs in the laughing, sparkling brook was much more delightful than peering through the shop windows at things which he wanted but could not purchase, and romping in the back pasture with Towser was more like sport than an hour spent on the street in the vicinity of Baker's Court.

In addition to his desire to be at home once more, was the fact that when his father arrived a certain scheme, to which he had given no slight amount of thought, might possibly be put into execution.

Therefore his heart was very light when, with valise in hand, he entered the stuffy kitchen of Mrs. Bartlett's home for the last time.

After the meal came to an end, Bob said laughingly, as he went toward the window : —

" Look out here."

Josiah obeyed, and saw ranged either side of the court, in true military precision, ten boys headed by Master Foss, all of them standing with their eyes fixed upon the door of the building.

" What are they doin' here ? " Josiah asked in surprise. " Bill don't think that we've got time to go anywhere with him, does he ? "

" Oh, no, he's only come to 'scort you down to the ferry in style."

Josiah looked distressed.

Since his experience in the station-house he did not wish to attract any more attention than was absolutely necessary, and was eager only to meet his father in the quietest possible manner.

" I think it would be a good deal better if we should go alone," he said after a long pause.

" So do I ; but there don't seem to be any way out of it. Bill is reckonin' on doin' this thing in great shape, an' I s'pose we'll have to let him run it, 'less you're willin' to tell him right up an' up that we oughter go alone."

"I wouldn't like to do that." Josiah replied slowly.

"Neither would I."

"What'er we goin' to do 'bout it?"

"You'd better go down, an' see what he's got to say. P'rhaps there'll be some way outer it."

Josiah, followed by Tom and Bob, descended to the court, and instantly the former appeared, a loud shout went up from the escort, thus showing what they were prepared to do when Mr. Shindle should arrive.

"Well, what do you think of it?" Bill asked proudly, as he approached Josiah.

"Think of what?"

"This crowd. I reckon your father'll be 'bout tickled to death when we give three cheers the minute he steps off the cars. Folks'll think he's the Governor by the time we get through yellin'."

"But I don't b'lieve the people at the station will want you screechin' 'round there."

"They'll have to be mighty smart if they can stop us after we once get started. I've figgered the whole thing out, same's it's done when a politician comes inter town, an' you needn't be 'fraid but we'll do it right up in style."

"See here, Bill, what makes you do so?" Josiah asked almost piteously, not feeling exactly at liberty to put a decided veto upon the scheme.

"What makes me? Why, we're countin' on comin' up to your farm next summer, an' wanter make it lively now for your father, so's he'll be glad to see us when we get there."

"I'm 'fraid mother hasn't got beds enough for all hands."

"That don't make a mite of difference; we're willin' to sleep on the hay, or anywhere. Tom acted as if he thought we counted on follerin' you 'round town; but of course we wouldn't do a thing like that. We'll jest start the old man in right, an' then he an' you can go wherever you wanter; but we're bound to see him first."

It surely seemed as if this settled the matter, so far as Master Shindle was concerned. If Bill was "bound" to carry out the programme he had arranged, then it would be but a waste of words to remonstrate with him, and Josiah remained silent.

"You'll have to let 'em go," Bob whispered, and

the young gentleman from Berry's Corner nodded his head with an air of resignation.

"I don't think you'd better do any yellin'," Tom said after a pause. "You see, Bill, some of them fellers at the station might kick up a fuss, an' it wouldn't look well if you should get 'rested the very minute Mr. Shindle struck the city, 'cause then there wouldn't be any chance of gettin' 'quainted with him."

"I'll risk their catchin' me," Master Foss replied boldly; but it was evident that the suggestion had aroused a certain train of thought which might result in the abandonment of at least a portion of the reception ceremonies.

By this time the escort had cast aside their martial bearing, and all were clustered around Josiah, urging him to leave the court as soon as possible.

"You see, there may be a block down on Broadway, an' it'll take us quite a while to get along, 'cause we're goin' to march reg'lar, same's soldiers do," one of the party suggested, and the visitor felt decidedly embarrassed at being made thus conspicuous.

"I reckon it'll have to be done, an' we might as

well have it over with at once." Tom whispered,
and the company set out in the order prescribed by
Master Foss.

Josiah walked arm in arm with Tom and Bob,
while on either side were five of the escort, with
Bill leading, and turning now and then to make
certain his men were in proper line.

It had been the intention of the Master of Ceremonies to conduct his party through the streets;
but before they had proceeded two blocks, its military formation was broken up, owing to the recklessness of the driver of a dray, and then he concluded it would be quite as well to march on the
sidewalk, even though the pedestrians were incon-
venienced thereby.

Josiah did not enjoy what Bill had arranged as
a triumphal procession for the boy whose guest he
intended to be during the following summer; but
when seeing that they attracted no slight amount
of attention, Tom and Bob concluded Master
Foss's idea was a thoroughly good one.

That Bill did not intend to do things in any
slipshod fashion, was shown by the fact that he
bought ferry tickets for the entire party, regardless

of the expense, and once on the Jersey City side of the river, ranged his followers in two ranks in front of the gate through which Mr. Shindle must emerge.

Fully an hour did Josiah and his many friends remain at the station; and after this long, weary time of waiting, Farmer Shindle, dressed in his best clothes, and looking as radiant as a boy with a ticket for the circus, stepped from the cars to be greeted more than warmly by his son.

"Well, well, well, and are you ready to go home?" the farmer asked, as if in surprise that the heir of the Shindle estate should show so much joy when his visit was about to come to an end.

"Yes indeed, father."

"Why, what's the matter? Haven't you had a tolerably good time?"

"Splendid! I've seen everything I ever heard about, an' a good deal more; but I ain't sorry to go back to you, an' mother, an' the calf, an' Towser."

"Well, well, well, now I'm glad to hear that," and Farmer Shindle laid his hand affectionately on Josiah's shoulder. "I feered you'd be wantin' to stay all winter, an' that would have pretty nigh broke me up. But here's Tom and Bob," and the good man turned to shake hands with the representatives of Baker's Court as he looked at them critically, and added. "You've lost that healthy coat of tan you got out to Berry's Corner last summer, boys. Next year I reckon we'll have to make farmers of both you little rascals, an' then you won't be layin' 'round this dreadful wicked city lookin' as peaked as sick chickens. But say, Josiah, does all this crowd belong to you?"

On hearing himself thus referred to, Bill Foss stepped quickly forward, and Josiah introduced him by saying : —

"This is a friend of Tom's and Bob's, father. He's been 'round with us a good deal, an' come down so's to make it kinder lively for you."

" Yes, sir, an' I brought them fellers with me," Bill said as he pointed to the escort. " You see, we didn't want you to land here without there was a reg'lar delegation to take care of you."

" Bless my soul !" the farmer exclaimed, as he looked at the two lines of boys, who were standing stiff as statues now they were being inspected.

"There wasn't any need of makin' a splurge for me, 'cause you see I'm only a plain old farmer, an' wouldn't know how to act if there was too much goin' on."

"But this thing had to be done," Bill explained, scowling furiously at a boy in the escort who chanced to step out of the line for an instant in order to save himself from being run over by a dray. "We're comin' out to see you next summer, you know, an' it seems like we oughter get 'quainted first."

"Comin' out to the farm, eh?"

"That's what we 'low to do," Bill replied decidedly.

"The whole crowd?"

"Yes sir'ee; we've 'greed to save up cash enough to buy tickets for all hands."

"Well," Farmer Shindle said hesitatingly. "there'll be plenty of room for you daytimes, an' I reckon we'll manage to have all you can eat; but I don't know as to stowin' you away at night. We'll have to talk with mother 'bout that."

"Don't you worry for us," Bill replied without hesitation. "We'll fix ourselves, an' all you've got to do is to have the farm right where it was when Tom an' Bob was out there."

"Did you invite all these boys to visit with you, Josiah?" the farmer asked in a whisper; and, in the fewest possible words, his son explained the situation of affairs.

"Oh, that's it, eh? Well, I wouldn't like to begrudge anything to these poor children who don't ever have a chance to get a breath of pure air: but at the same time, I ain't sure as it would be treatin' mother jest right to have all of 'em pilin' in on her in such a load."

Bill waited until the whispered conversation had come to an end, and then said in a confidential tone to Josiah: —

"I reckon you had better go now, 'cause you'll wanter see your father; but we'll meet you agin before the train leaves."

"I guess that would be the best way," the boy replied, thoroughly relieved at the prospect of parting with the escort.

"We ain't goin' to lose sight of you, Mr. Shindle," Bill said to the farmer: "but we've got a little business over on this side of the river, an' will turn up agin to-night. You'll get along without us, 'cause Tom and Bob can put you 'round."

"I reckon we shall get through all right." the farmer replied with a laugh, and Bill gave the word of command to take up the line of march in a very loud voice.

Josiah was more than willing to part with these acquaintances; and after watching Bill and his friends until they had passed through the gate to the street, he turned to his father.

It was some moments before Mr. Shindle was ready to go on board the ferry-boat, because of the questions which Tom and Bob thought necessary to ask concerning the farm; and when they were seated on the steamer where Josiah could talk unreservedly, owing to the fact that his friends were, perforce, some distance away, he asked seriously : —

" Does it cost much to keep a boy or a girl about my age ? "

" Well, now, that depends." the farmer replied as he rubbed his chin reflectively : " if they were to be kept the year 'round. I reckon what they'd take from the table wouldn't be missed : but when it comes to fillin' 'em up for a week, they get away with an amazin' power of vittles — not that I be-grudge what a person eats at our house, though," he added quickly.

"Would it cost a great deal to keep a child like me?"

"That depends. You never was a careful boy with shoe-leather, Josiah, an' don't take so kindly to work as I wish you did. Now, them Berry youngsters will stay in the field all day long with never a whimper; but you no sooner weed two or three rows than you're done, and want to skylark in the woods, catchin' turtles, or somethin' like that. There's a good many times that a boy's a heap of trouble, even if you don't count the expense."

"I'm talkin' of a girl, father."

Up to this moment Farmer Shindle probably thought the questions were asked from motives of curiosity; and now the good man turned squarely around in his seat as he looked at the boy earnestly, and asked: —

"What have you got in your head, Josiah?"

This was not exactly the time when Master Shindle intended to present the story of the match-girl. He had expected to bring his father gradually up to the point where he could propose, without exciting too much astonishment, that she be invited to the farm for a long visit.

It was not possible to further prepare him for what was coming, however, and he plunged boldly into the matter by telling all he knew about the child who sold matches on Chatham Square.

Very pathetically he described her lonely life and home, with no one but a drunken woman to care for her; the pinched, wan face, and the hardships necessarily endured while trying to earn a livelihood on the streets during the winter season, until, from the varying expression of his father's features, Josiah knew he had excited sympathy, if nothing more.

The good man wiped his forehead vigorously as if excessively warm, and said in a tone of mingled bewilderment and regret: —

" I wish you hadn't told me this, Josiah, till you had talked with mother. I was countin' on seein' a good bit of the city to-day; but somehow your story has taken all the fun outer me."

" Why not carry her home with us, father? If

mother isn't willin' she needn't stay any longer'n Tom an' Bob did, an' the poor little thing will be jest so much the better for havin' a chance to live two or three days like decent folks."

" But there's the expense of takin' her back an' forth, 'Siah. Don't forget that, for your mother won't."

" I've got enough to pay for the ticket. I was goin' to buy you an' mother somethin': but I know you'd be willin' to get along without the presents for the sake of givin' her a good time."

Farmer Shindle was so deeply engaged with his thoughts that he made no reply to this last suggestion of his son's, until the ferry-boat touched the slip with a shock which caused him considerable alarm, and as the young gentlemen from Baker's Court led the way to the street, he said : —

" Let's go right up an' see that girl. If she wants to go out to the farm for a week, an' you're willin' to pay the fares, I don't see as there's any reason for sayin' no. Mother can't be very much opposed to it, 'cause the harvestin's over, the apples are dried, an' she's through preservin'. I'll risk it anyhow."

This was as much as Josiah had dared to hope for, and now had come the time when he could tell Tom and Bob of the plan.

" Well, that's what I call a big thing," Master Green said in a tone of approbation. " It's goin' to be tough on Sadie to stay out-doors all winter jest to earn what little she needs, an' if you folks take care of her, she'll be mighty lucky."

Both the boys were as excited and delighted by the information as if it had been a scheme devised for their especial benefit.

They led the way to Chatham Square at a rapid pace, hurrying Farmer Shindle across the street amid the press of vehicles. until the poor man was almost certain he would never live to reach the desired spot, owing to the recklessness of his guides.

There was no difficulty in finding Sadie.

She was standing where Josiah first saw her, and this time he did not hesitate to approach.

" Say, wouldn't you like to go out to Berry's Corner an' live with father, an' mother, an' me ? " he cried eagerly, as he halted in front of her. while Tom and Bob pressed close behind to hear every word of the conversation. "I'm goin' home to-night, an' we'll take you for a week, anyhow; then perhaps mother'll let you stay a good while longer. It's ever so much nicer out there than it is in the city."

The child was bewildered by Josiah's impetuous manner, as well as by the proposition so hastily made, and appeared wholly at a loss for an answer.

Then Tom, who fancied some recommendation from him might be necessary, described the Shindle farm, told of his visit of the previous year, and painted so eloquently in words a picture of the life at Berry's Corner, that soon Sadie was as excited as any of the party.

At this point Mr. Shindle took part in the conversation.

The child had aroused his sympathies, and he now felt as eager to take her home as did Josiah.

"We haven't got any little girl out to our house," he said, holding the tiny hand in his hard palm, "an' I know mother would take you right into her heart. She's a bit close-fisted at times, 'cause we have to count every cent to make both ends meet; but in five minutes after you strike

the house she'll be as if you was her own. The good Book says there ain't a sparrow falls without the Father's notice, an' He counts on our doin' all we can to prevent the fallin', so I reckon it'll be layin' up treasure for the hereafter to take you home."

Sadie did not exactly understand what the old gentleman was saying so earnestly; but she knew it all meant an invitation to visit the farm, and little persuasion was needed to gain her consent.

Just then Master Bartlett took charge of the matter by adding : —

" I'll go down to Mother Hunter's with her, an see that she's ready to leave with you an' Josiah, Mr. Shindle. When it's time to start, we'll be waitin' for you at the court."

CHAPTER XVII.

AT HOME.

THIS arrangement was immediately carried into effect, because Tom did not wait for an expression of opinion regarding it.

He led Sadie across the square, and the other members of the party were left alone, Farmer Shindle saying, when the child was hidden from view by the throng of pedestrians: —

" You've done a good deed, 'Siah, no matter what mother says. It's a burnin' shame for that poor little thing to have to earn her livin' sellin' matches on the street. I'll pay for the railroad tickets, an' you can spend your money as you like." Then, conscious of having obeyed a kindly impulse, and feeling better because of it, the farmer bethought himself of the plans he had made for enjoying this brief visit, and asked, " Ain't there a wax figger show somewhere 'round here ? "

" Yes, sir," Bob replied. " I know of a big one way up town ; but it costs fifty cents to go in."

" I don't care if they tax six shillings apiece, we're goin' with the whole crowd. It's the first time I've been in the city with nothin' to do, for more'n two years. I've begun by agreein' to pay that little girl's way out home, an' I guess I can stand three or four dollars more. Show us where it is, Bob, an' I'll buy the tickets."

Under Master Green's guidance the party walked toward Broadway until Farmer Shindle remembered that Tom was in danger of losing his share of the sight-seeing, and suddenly halted as he said : —

" Now look here, I don't like to cheat that Bartlett boy outer the fun while he's helpin' the little girl. S'pose you run after him, Bob? 'Siah an' me'll see enough right here on this corner to keep us amused till you get back, for it ain't often we have sich a chance."

Bob, who had been regretting his partner's absence, was more than willing to act upon the suggestion, and set out at full speed, in order to economize time.

So intent was Josiah and his father on the scenes around them, that it hardly seemed more than five minutes before the boys returned, both looking radiantly happy because of the good fortune in store for Sadie.

Although Mr. Shindle's destination was the "wax figure show" on Twenty-Third street, considerable time was occupied in reaching the place, for he found it necessary to stop here and there, and look about him quite as often as had Josiah.

Tom and Bob piloted the party directly up Broadway, doing the utmost to keep their guests in motion; for now that his father was with him, it seemed as if Josiah's exclamations of delight were louder and more frequent than before.

The pedestrians enjoyed the odd antics of these Berry Corner pleasure-seekers to such an extent, that before the party had reached Bleecker street the attention which they received was even more apparent than Bob and Tom fancied desirable.

"We'll have to hurry the old man along faster'n this," the former said in a whisper, "else we'll have the whole city taggin' after us. He's actin' worse'n Josiah ever dared to, an' how it'll be when we get up among the swell stores. I don't know."

"I reckon it would be a good idea to holler fire, when he gets so much of a crowd 'round him." Tom suggested. "Perhaps if we did that we could run him pretty near all the way up."

"I don't b'lieve it would work, 'cause he'd soon find out there wasn't anything the matter, an' we don't want to make the old man mad. He was too good last summer for us to play any funny business."

"Then tell him if we don't get there pretty soon, the show'll be closed. That'll settle it."

Bob did as his friend suggested; and the possibility that he might lose the opportunity of seeing this exhibition, of which he had read and heard so much, caused Mr. Shindle to accelerate his pace, greatly to the delight of his guides.

The old gentleman walked rapidly several moments, and then they had arrived in front of a toy-store.

Here he came to a full halt; and it is questionable if even a genuine alarm of fire would have caused him to move on, unless, by chance, the engine had passed within sight.

He appeared to take as much pleasure in looking at the toy soldiers, dolls, and miniature base-ball outfits as did Josiah; and the two flattened their noses against the window in blissful ignorance of the amusement they were affording the spectators.

Mr. Shindle compared the toys with such as he had owned when he was a child, and speculated with Josiah as to what he would buy for Sadie if he was possessed of unlimited means, until one would have found it difficult, judging simply from the conversation, to say which was the elder of the two.

"I reckon your mother would go jest about wild if she was to see a thing like this," Mr. Shindle said, when Bob had tried in vain several moments to induce him to continue the journey up town.

"I wish you'd brought her with you," Josiah replied. "You can't think how many things I've seen that I knew both she an' you'd like, since I've been here, an' it seemed too bad we couldn't all have been together."

"I did ask her if she wouldn't come down; but she's forever thinkin' about how much the railroad ticket costs; an' while I don't want to make any complaint against your mother, Josiah, I must say she's a master hand at figgerin' how many cents there are in a dollar, so I don't know as we've got any call to blame her. You see, for a good many years we had an up-hill row to hoe, an' she's buckled down to it so long, that now when we're a little fore-handed, she can't get free of them ways of scrimpin'."

In due course of time, Bob's and Tom's efforts were rewarded with success, and the little party moved on, slowly to be sure, but, as Bob said, they were "headin' the right way," and it was only a question of an hour or more when they would arrive at their destination.

Bill Foss could not have been more jaunty in his manner, even when making his best efforts to do honor to Josiah in order to pave the way for the summer's visit, than was Mr. Shindle when he stepped in front of the ticket-office at the "wax-figure show," and purchased the cards of admission.

"It's a good deal of money to pay out for two or three hour's fun," he said in a confidential tone

to the gentleman in the box-office, as the latter returned three dollars in change for a five, accompanying them with four bits of pasteboard which would
pass the party by the Cerberus at the door: "but
you see when a man don't come down to the city
more'n once in two years, I reckon he can afford
it."

This explanation of his almost criminal prodi-
gality had the effect of soothing the farmer's
mind, so far as the expenditure of two dollars was
concerned, and the four entered the museum in
open-mouthed astonishment.

This was a place which neither Tom nor Bob
had ever visited before, owing to the high price of
admission; and they were quite as much delighted
as were their country friends, although both took
especial care to prevent giving such palpable evidences of their enjoyment.

In a very few moments the young gentlemen of
Newspaper Row were wearied with looking at the
figures of celebrities, and Bob said confidently to
his companion : —

"I don't understand how it is they charge half
a dollar jest to come in here and see these people.

I can find a good many more on Broadway any day;" and it is very likely they would have voted this particular exhibition a failure, when taken in connection with the amount charged for admission, had it not been that Josiah accidentally found his way down the staircase to the Chamber of Horrors.

He came back swiftly, his eyes gleaming with astonishment, his face almost pale, and exclaimed in a voice trembling with surprise and emotion : —

" Come down here quick! They're murderin' folks, an' hangin' 'em, an' everything else! It's awful nice!"

Tom and Bob had nothing more to say about the entrance fee, for here was an opportunity to drink their fill of horrors.

During the next fifteen minutes not a single member of the party spoke, as they walked from one scene to another in what was really like silent fear.

" This is an awful wicked world," Farmer Shindle said solemnly, when he had fully understood the seven stages of the burglar's life, " an' if ever the time comes when I get tired stayin' out to

Berry's Corner, I'll come right down here. It's enough to make a man wish there never was such places as cities. Say, Bob, do you s'pose them figgers are all **wax**, or are they reg'lar skins stuffed?"

Master Green should have acknowledged that he was unable to answer this question, but it seemed hardly the proper thing for him to confess his ignorance, and he replied gravely: —

"I reckon some of 'em's wax, an' some of 'em ain't. I'm pretty certain that feller what's goin' to have his head cut off is a reg'lar man stuffed. I s'pose they glued him together after the choppin' was over."

This made the scene of the guillotine more realistic, and the little party paused in front of the terrible picture until Mr. Shindle said with a sigh: —

"It's no use, boys. I've got enough of this sort of thing, even if it did cost half a dollar apiece. I reckon we'd better go out on the street where we can see somethin' more lively. If there's any chance 'round here to get a bite to eat, I wouldn't mind payin' for a cup of coffee an' a fried cake."

"There's lots of places like that," Bob said

quickly : for the idea of having a lunch at an up-
town restaurant was even more entrancing than anything to be found in the museum.

Ten minutes later the four were seated at a mar-
ble-topped table. which Mr. Shindle thought out of
place in such an establishment. since, as he said.
" wood would have done jest as well so long as it
was made strong enough to hold the feed. an'
wouldn't have come nearly so expensive."

Josiah's father generously allowed his guests to
order what they wished. and this was done without
reference to the bill of fare.

A thoroughly enjoyable lunch it was until the
check had been brought. and then the amount
caused even more consternation than had the one
at Coney Island among the chowder-eaters.

The farmer looked at it a moment in eloquent
silence. and then said, as he plunged his hand with
a certain deliberation into his pocket : —

" I reckon it's jest as well for me that I don't
come to the city very often. 'cordin' to the price
we're gettin' for potatoes now. I don't groan over
payin' two dollars to go into a show like the one
we jest come out of : but when they can figger up

a dollar and seventy-five cents for two or three mouthfuls such as we've had, it strikes me we're goin' it pretty strong, eh, Josiah?"

"Things are awful expensive in the city, father. I've found that out since I've been here;" and then the heir of the Shindle estate told of the amount spent at Coney Island, until his father began to look upon Messrs. Green and Bartlett as capitalists. if they could afford to entertain their guests in such a manner.

"It's no use to cry over spilled milk, so I won't say anything more about it; but it'll be a long day before I set down to a dollar and seventy-five cent meal agin."

Then it seemed as if the farmer put from his mind all idea of the value of money, and from that hour until the day's pleasuring had come to an end, there was not a moment which had in it less than sixty full seconds of perfect enjoyment.

Farmer Shindle not only invited the boys to several other places of interest, but purchased peanuts and candy with the recklessness of a spendthrift, until there was every probability the entire party would need strong doses of Jamaica ginger before morning.

The inhabitants of Baker's Court were in a ferment of excitement when the amusement-seekers finally returned.

All were acquainted with the little match-girl, and more than once had they discussed the possibility of doing something to aid her for whom the battle of life had begun so early; but thus far nothing had been accomplished.

Instantly word was brought of the farmer's generous invitation, however, every mother in the vicinity bent all her energies toward replenishing Sadie's scanty wardrobe; and when Mr. Shindle and the boys arrived, she presented a much neater and more cleanly appearance than ever since Tom had known her.

Josiah purchased for his mother a lace cap that he thought a marvel of beauty because of the bright red ribbons with which it was tied. In making the selection he was aided by his father, who told him, as if it was a great secret, that when his mother was young she always wore red, therefore there could be no mistake if he selected a head covering plentifully bedecked with this color.

Fifty cents more of his rapidly diminishing capital had been invested in a gaudily-painted but not very serviceable whip for his father, and thus Josiah was to carry home gifts despite his charitable scheme.

Then the huge valise was brought down-stairs, and Farmer Shindle said, as he seized it by the leathern handles:—

" We'll take good care of the little girl, neighbors, an' next summer, if mother an' me are spared, I reckon the crops will be big enough so's we can stand the feed of a dozen youngsters from 'round here, who I allow don't see a spear of grass from one year's end to another."

One afternoon in December, when snow covered the brown earth with a mantle of whiteness, as the sleek, well-fed cows and horses were housed in the warm barn, munching contentedly the hay gathered for their especial benefit, and all Nature was under the Ice King's rule, the Shindle family, with the match-girl in their midst, sat before a roaring fire in the rag-carpeted kitchen, enjoying the genial warmth all the more because of the intense cold outside.

During fully ten minutes not a word had been spoken; and then the farmer said as he laid his hand on the head of the tiny girl, who was sitting upon a footstool near Mrs. Shindle's side, learning to knit:—

"It would have been pretty hard lines, mother, if this little thing was obliged to walk the streets of that great, big city tryin' to earn money enough for her feed."

"Indeed it would, father, and while we live she shall never again know what it is to be homeless," the good woman replied, as she stroked the brown hair of the little head which had dropped into her lap to hide the tears of gratitude.

Happy and contented as were all the inmates of the kitchen, there was a certain huskiness in the farmer's voice as he added:—

"After all, mother, it ain't givin' we are, it's receivin', because she gives more'n she takes. I reckon when 'Siah an' me lugged her away from New York, it was cuttin' a mighty big coupon from them five shares of the fresh-air fund we invested in last summer."

THE END.